THE ART OF EAVESDROPPING

THE SIDEKICK'S SURVIVAL GUIDE, BOOK 1

CHRISTY BARRITT

To my friend Gina, who always entertains me with her stories about being a Filipino in America.

To my friend Helza, who inspired me with stories of growing up in Peru.

To my friends Rachel and Curtis, who served as missionaries in Ecuador and showed me what it was like to have a heart for those overseas.

COMPLETE BOOK LIST

Squeaky Clean Mysteries:
  #1 Hazardous Duty
  #2 Suspicious Minds
  #2.5 It Came Upon a Midnight Crime (novella)
  #3 Organized Grime
  #4 Dirty Deeds
  #5 The Scum of All Fears
  #6 To Love, Honor and Perish
  #7 Mucky Streak
  #8 Foul Play
  #9 Broom & Gloom
  #10 Dust and Obey
  #11 Thrill Squeaker
  #11.5 Swept Away (novella)
  #12 Cunning Attractions
  #13 Cold Case: Clean Getaway

#14 Cold Case: Clean Sweep

#15 Cold Case: Clean Break

#16 Cleans to an End (coming soon)

While You Were Sweeping, A Riley Thomas Spinoff

The Sierra Files:
#1 Pounced

#2 Hunted

#3 Pranced

#4 Rattled

The Gabby St. Claire Diaries (a Tween Mystery series):
The Curtain Call Caper

The Disappearing Dog Dilemma

The Bungled Bike Burglaries

The Worst Detective Ever
#1 Ready to Fumble

#2 Reign of Error

#3 Safety in Blunders

#4 Join the Flub

#5 Blooper Freak

#6 Flaw Abiding Citizen

#7 Gaffe Out Loud

#8 Joke and Dagger

#9 Wreck the Halls

#10 Glitch and Famous (coming soon)

Raven Remington

Relentless 1

Relentless 2 (coming soon)

Holly Anna Paladin Mysteries:

#1 Random Acts of Murder

#2 Random Acts of Deceit

#2.5 Random Acts of Scrooge

#3 Random Acts of Malice

#4 Random Acts of Greed

#5 Random Acts of Fraud

#6 Random Acts of Outrage

#7 Random Acts of Iniquity

Lantern Beach Mysteries

#1 Hidden Currents

#2 Flood Watch

#3 Storm Surge

#4 Dangerous Waters

#5 Perilous Riptide

#6 Deadly Undertow

Lantern Beach Romantic Suspense

Tides of Deception

Shadow of Intrigue

Storm of Doubt

Winds of Danger

Rains of Remorse

Lantern Beach P.D.

On the Lookout
Attempt to Locate
First Degree Murder
Dead on Arrival
Plan of Action

Lantern Beach Escape

Afterglow (a novelette)

Lantern Beach Blackout

Dark Water
Safe Harbor
Ripple Effect
Rising Tide

The Sidekick's Survival Guide

The Art of Eavesdropping
The Perks of Meddling
The Skill of Snooping (coming soon)
The Practice of Prying (coming soon)

Carolina Moon Series

Home Before Dark
Gone By Dark
Wait Until Dark
Light the Dark
Taken By Dark

Suburban Sleuth Mysteries:

Death of the Couch Potato's Wife

Fog Lake Suspense:
Edge of Peril
Margin of Error
Brink of Danger
Line of Duty

Cape Thomas Series:
Dubiosity
Disillusioned
Distorted

Standalone Romantic Mystery:
The Good Girl

Suspense:
Imperfect
The Wrecking

Sweet Christmas Novella:
Home to Chestnut Grove

Standalone Romantic-Suspense:
Keeping Guard
The Last Target
Race Against Time
Ricochet
Key Witness

Lifeline

High-Stakes Holiday Reunion

Desperate Measures

Hidden Agenda

Mountain Hideaway

Dark Harbor

Shadow of Suspicion

The Baby Assignment

The Cradle Conspiracy

Trained to Defend

Nonfiction:

Characters in the Kitchen

Changed: True Stories of Finding God through Christian Music (out of print)

The Novel in Me: The Beginner's Guide to Writing and Publishing a Novel (out of print)

CHAPTER ONE

I used to feel I had the whole world in front of me. Now, I was certain that it wasn't the actual world, but a mirage showing what my life could have looked like.

So, instead of looking ahead, I decided to glance behind me.

Like, I *literally* peered back. As in, into my rearview mirror at the street stretching there.

I couldn't help but feel like my past was trailing me like a piece of toilet paper unknowingly stuck on my shoe.

Though nothing suspicious caught my eye, my gut told me someone was following me.

But what sense would that make?

I was Elliot Ransom. An introvert. The new girl in town. Someone who prided herself in being fluent in English, Spanish, and Nerd.

In other words, I wasn't a threat—not unless I was at a spelling bee.

I sighed and turned my gaze back to the road ahead. It was my first day on a new job, and the bright, sunny spring weather seemed to hold promise.

I'd take whatever hope I could hold on to.

Nothing had felt right since I'd moved away from the Amazon village where I'd grown up to this hoity-toity Virginia city that masqueraded as a wholesome river town. For a goal-oriented twenty-seven-year-old, the change had been traumatic, and lately I'd eaten away my troubles with subpar mangoes and canned pineapple.

I missed the cheerful sounds of the jungle in the morning.

The clean, dewy air.

The love of my life, Sergio.

Mostly, I missed feeling excited about the prospects of my future. Instead, I'd been transported to this new place and left with the realization that home was no longer attainable.

And it never again would be.

I glanced behind me one more time. Still nothing suspicious caught my eye.

But the gut feeling remained, a feeling that had been finely tuned by my father, Eduardo Lucas Eldorado Topeka de Torres. Yes, our last names were different, but that was a story for another day.

Just then, my car sputtered. Smoke rose from the hood. The vehicle lurched.

I pulled off to the side of the road, where my sedan—a

silver Buick with a red door—died faster than my social life as of late.

With a sigh, I climbed out, popped the hood, and propped it open. Then I stared at all the car engine components in front of me, trying to figure out what might have possibly gone wrong, causing smoke to come out.

I knew a lot of things, but I had no clue how to fix a car.

I pressed my fingers against my temples as my head began to throb. *This is not the time for weakness. It's time to operate at peakness.*

When I got nervous, I started to rhyme. The habit was weird, but it was all mine. As I'd gotten older, it sounded less cute and more like a wannabe half-Hispanic, half-Caucasian rapper.

I tried to start the car again. The engine clicked but refused to turn over.

I had to think here. I had exactly six dollars and thirty-four cents in my wallet. No credit cards. And a dead car.

Not to mention that this was my first day at my new job. Being late would be a horrible first impression. I knew I shouldn't have taken this new position. I should have stuck with my old, boring job as an insurance specialist.

Just then, a car pulled behind me. It wasn't just any car either. The Bentley probably cost more than I would make in a decade.

My jaw tightened when I saw the man who climbed out and strode toward me. He wore a white suit and expensive sunglasses that made him appear important—not exactly the kind of guy who stopped on the side of the road to help someone with a clunker like mine. More like the type who hired people to iron his underwear and separate his M&Ms by color.

"Looks like you're having some problems." He paused beside me. "Is there anything I can do to help?"

"I'm not really sure what happened," I started, the words coming out too fast. "I was just driving down the road when I saw the smoke and heard a strange sound."

The man pushed his sunglasses up to the top of his gelled dark hair, revealing beautiful brown eyes. As he fiddled under the hood, I couldn't help but worry he'd get grease on his crisp, white suit.

My dad had taught me to always be observant. He'd told me it might save my life one day. I'd never forgotten that. During the beginnings of the political uprisings in my country, my father had given me survival tips instead of telling nighttime stories.

And that was why I had trouble relating to so many people around me. Though my family had frequently taken trips to the States, my upbringing wasn't like most people's.

"Oh, here it is." My Knight-in-White-Armani fiddled with something before looking back at me. "Do me a favor and start the engine. Let's see what happens."

I climbed back into the car and did as he said. As I turned the key in the ignition, my engine purred to life. Relief rushed through me. Maybe there *was* hope for the rest of my life—I mean, day.

Quickly, I climbed from the car and met the man. "Thank you so much."

He stepped back and grinned, his teeth gleaming like snow on a sunny day. "It's no problem. It looks like one of the spark plug wires became disconnected. You still might want to take it into a garage, just to make sure. But this should get you to where you're going, provided it's not too far away."

"I can't tell you how much I appreciate this." I offered a grateful smile. This guy, despite his snooty appearance, really had been a lifesaver.

The man pulled his sunglasses back over his eyes and flashed that million-dollar grin again. "It's no problem. Helping out a beautiful damsel in distress is the least I can do." With one more wave, he strode back to his car. "¡Mantente alerta!"

I froze.

What had he just said? Certainly I'd misunderstood.

Because it had sounded like he said, "mantente alerta."

Spanish for "Stay alert."

A phrase my father had often used.

That couldn't be a coincidence.

The uneasy feeling returned to me. Had that man been following me? What sense would that make?

I glanced at my watch again before climbing back into my car and heading down the road. With any luck, I'd show up for my first day on the job right on time.

But I couldn't shake the notion that something bad was speeding toward me like a jaguar closing in on its prey.

After getting stuck behind every red light, I rolled into work ten minutes late. I paused in front of the office to gather myself before going inside. The building was a storefront located one block back from the quaint tourist area along the beautiful Storm River. The outside was painted robin's egg blue, and cheerful white shutters hung on either side of the wide windows.

It looked welcoming and warm, at least.

When I finally walked into the office building of Driscoll and Associates, a private investigation firm, I noticed that I'd somehow managed to get a streak of grease on my new blouse.

While the man who'd helped me with my car walked away totally clean. Go figure.

Instead of changing, I buttoned my pale-yellow sweater, trying to hide the evidence so I could look professional. Impressions were 90 percent of success. Another tidbit from my dad.

By nature, I was the neat but comfortable kind. I had straight brown hair that wouldn't hold a curl. A boyish figure —no hips or chest. A no-frill way of dressing.

My dad had said that allowed my natural beauty to shine through.

Dads were supposed to say stuff like that.

I paused and glanced around the reception area. The place was decorated professionally with walnut-stained shiplap walls, rich wood floors, and sleek furniture. The scent of sandalwood floated in the air, and electricity seemed to zing through the atmosphere.

I smiled at the woman at the front desk. "I'm Elliot Ransom, and I'm here to see Mr. Driscoll."

A blonde with big hair, full lips, and oversized glasses unapologetically studied me. "You must be the new girl."

First impression: Ditzy. Slightly vain. A talker. From the Deep South, based on her drawl.

"That's me. Elliot Ransom."

She flashed a smile that didn't quite reach her eyes. "Maybe you'll make it longer than the last one did."

What did that mean? I didn't know much about my new boss. I'd read an online ad stating he was looking for an assistant. He paid considerably higher than what I'd been paid at my old job, and the position sounded entirely more interesting.

"Velma!" A deep voice rattled the room from a doorway in the distance. "Is she here yet?"

Velma's eyes widened, and she sat up straighter in her chair. Her hand flew out and knocked some papers from the desk. The pile fluttered to the floor like feathers in duck-hunting season. Instead of picking them up, her fingers splayed across the desk as if hanging on for dear life.

"Yes, sir. I'm sending her right in." Velma looked at me with wide eyes beneath her purple-framed glasses before whispering, "Good luck."

I hadn't remembered my new boss being quite as scary when I'd met him for my interview. Then again, we'd only talked for five minutes in-between press interviews he gave in front of City Hall. His job opening ad had stated he wanted someone detail-oriented who spoke fluent Spanish, liked to read Agatha Christie, and wasn't PC.

It was like the ad was written for me. I was bilingual, loved mystery novels, and hated personal computers. I was more of a Mac girl.

Mostly, what I remembered was the man had smelled like cigars and bloated self-worth. Oscar Driscoll had asked a few questions, looked me over, and then told me I was hired. Maybe that did seem a little suspicious, but desperation won over complaining. I was *so* over my job at the insurance company.

I stepped into the office and spotted my new boss sitting behind his massive desk—a desk built for such a person. The man was large and imposing, with a round face, a nearly bald head, and an awful mustache below his shiny, bulbous nose. He looked to be in his early fifties, and, based on the dish on his desk, he liked pistachios.

He had helped solve the highly publicized crime of the Ernesto family five years ago, and he'd become somewhat of a celebrity. Helena Ernesto had been accused of killing her husband, but Oscar found a key piece of evidence indicating Helena's brother was actually guilty.

Media coverage had been intense and constant, and Oscar had shone in the spotlight. Eventually, he'd even written a book about it, and a made-for-TV movie had been aired with some actor named Kevin James playing Oscar.

I'd done a little research on the man before coming today. The Type A in me couldn't resist.

He observed me for a moment before nodding. "Good. You're here. You're from South America, right?"

"That's right. I grew up in a town right on the edge of the jungle and—"

"You look Hispanic."

"I do, but my mom is actually American—"

"Say something in Spanish."

"In Spanish?" I repeated, feeling my lungs deflate.

"Did I stutter?"

I flinched at his sharp words and knew he meant business. Then I quickly blurted something in Spanish.

"What did you say?" he demanded.

I swallowed hard but refused to break eye contact. "That kindness always wins."

I'd actually said, "This man is prickly." Oscar didn't need to know that, though.

He slowly nodded in a way that made me feel like I was livestock being paraded before being butchered.

"Now act like you don't speak English," he barked.

I straightened my back, realizing this wasn't the job opportunity I'd been dreaming about. Role-playing hadn't been in the description. All kinds of internal alarms were sounding right now.

I took a step back. "I think this is a bad idea—"

"No, please." His voice softened, and he patted the air with his hands. "Just try it. I'll explain in a moment."

I let out a sigh, glanced at the door, and then decided to humor him for just another moment. After all, I'd already quit my old job. I needed another income. Maybe he had a really good reason for asking me to do this.

I blurted out another string of Spanish and made sure the words came out fast and that I used quick, frantic motions.

Translation: I don't know what you're saying, you big jerk. And I'm having second thoughts about your ethics, but I have a feeling you don't care.

A huge grin lit his face, and he nodded, leaning back in his chair as if I'd just passed his audition. "Perfect. You just need to avert your gaze more. Now, I need you to do a job for me."

"Sure. What is it? Filing? Running background checks? Doing some translation work on the Mac?" Paperwork was my specialty, as of late.

I could organize forms alphabetically with my eyes closed. I could label files until they were so pretty you wanted to cry. If there was a Heisman Trophy for office work, I felt certain I'd be a contender.

It was one of the reasons I'd excelled at my job back in Yerba. I'd been chief of staff for one of my province's legislators. He'd never missed a meeting or one of his staffers' birthdays—thanks to yours truly.

"I need you to go undercover."

I blinked, certain I'd heard him incorrectly. "Come again?"

I was pretty sure that qualification wasn't on my résumé. No, I'd listed clerical skills. Like an overwhelming and nerdish knowledge of Excel. Bragging rights on crafting irresistible press releases. Ability to process payroll with the dedication of an addict flying high on addition and subtraction.

None of which required subterfuge.

Oscar waved his thick finger in the air. "That's right. I knew you were *perfecto* when I hired you for this job." He said "perfecto" with the flare of an Italian who'd just made the perfect pasta dish.

I started to take a step back but stopped myself. "I'm not an actress. Call it a quirk, but I don't do that kind of work."

Oh, no. I was nervous. Those rhymes always gave it away. I turned into a less talented Dr. Seuss. If I'd written one of his books, it would go: *Oh, the places you'll end up. Some of them you will hate. But sometimes you need to understand that life isn't great.*

"You do now." Oscar pushed a folder toward me. "Everything you need to know is right in here in this dossier. Study it. You have a job to do tonight. An innocent man is counting on you, señorita. Now, *auf Wiedersehen.*"

Auf Wiedersehen? Oscar didn't think that was Spanish, did he? Because I was pretty sure that was German for goodbye.

Either way, I didn't like the sound of his words. What in the world could Oscar be getting at? I was about to find out.

Mantente alerta, I reminded myself. Stay alert.

Yes, Papa. I'd remain on guard.

But right now, I needed to remember everything my dad had ever taught me about survival.

CHAPTER TWO

After exiting Oscar's office, file in hand, I sat at a desk Velma had shown me to. Apparently, this would be my space during my tenure—however brief—at Driscoll and Associates.

There was no privacy here, just a glass wall behind the reception area. Another desk stood beside mine, and I wondered who it belonged to. I supposed I'd find out soon enough.

I still had so much to learn about this new town I'd moved to three months ago.

Storm River was located anywhere from forty-five minutes to three hours outside Washington, DC—depending on traffic. The city was situated, as you might have guessed, on a small river that branched from the Potomac. But this wasn't just any river. This river had a sandy beach, trendy restaurants, and a resort feel.

From what I understood during my brief stay, politicians from Washington liked to escape to the area on the weekends. Large homes had been built on the outskirts of town to house them. The area's original homes were bungalows, painted bright colors, with white picket fences and an all-American feel. The structures hearkened back to simpler times. Yet, for the simplicity, the town still felt strangely complicated.

Initially, I'd thought it was strange that a PI had set up shop in the small town as opposed to somewhere closer to the DC suburbs. But then I realized just how many people came and went on weekends. Not just any people. Powerful people. Politicians. Executives. People drenched in old money.

Then it all made sense. Oscar Driscoll had known this area offered a certain sense of privacy because of its distance from the DC Beltway. It was really quite smart, I supposed.

I flipped through the pages in the file my new boss had handed me. Oscar had been hired by a man named Flash "the Birdie" Slivinski, a professional golfer who'd been accused of murdering twenty-five-year-old Sarah Vance. Flash claimed he woke up in his condo and found Sarah dead on the floor beside him. Her throat had been slashed. He said he'd blacked out and had no idea what happened.

But he knew he wasn't a killer.

We needed to prove that.

The murder had happened a week ago, but Flash was out on bail until his trial date.

He'd been seen leaving a bar with Sarah, but Flash claimed he'd never talked to her before. He said the two had met for the first time that evening. They hit it off and had gone back to his place to get to know each other.

The last thing he remembered was talking to Sarah about a recent trip he'd taken to Paris. Then everything went black. The tox screen hadn't shown any drugs in his system, nor had he had any medical conditions that could have caused him to pass out.

Sarah Vance had worked as a cosmetics salesperson. She lived in Georgetown, right outside DC, and, because of her job, she traveled throughout the area to sell her products to various stores. She was originally from Nebraska, and she had long, honey-blonde hair, big eyes, and an overly confident smile. Interviews with friends, neighbors, and coworkers were included in the file, as well as a note saying that Oscar was working hand in hand with Flash's lawyer.

A handwritten note at the end made my eyes widen. "Your mission, if you choose to accept it, is . . ."

What did that mean? Another American pop culture reference perhaps? I really needed to learn more of those.

My eyes widened as I read the assignment. Then I read it again.

"I'm supposed to go undercover as a cleaning lady who doesn't speak English?" I blurted. "At the police station where the lead detective on the Sarah Vance case works?" Horror laced my words.

Velma looked back at me. My voice had obviously carried through the open glass door.

She frowned, the expression overblown but the sympathy appreciated.

"It's a great way to get information," she offered. Her dangling bracelets clanged together as she raised her hands in a shrug.

"I am going to be joining the afterhours cleaning crew," I continued, my gaze skimming the dossier, as Oscar had called it.

"You're going to be like a mole. A very clean mole."

"The animal?" What was she talking about?

She stared at me. "You know, a person planted inside an organization to gain knowledge of situations."

Another American expression.

"I'm supposed to spy on the police?" My mouth dropped open. This seemed like a very bad idea.

"Pretty much. We need to know what they know—especially the top-secret stuff."

I closed the folder and walked toward Velma, afraid that Oscar might overhear my question. "Is this normal? I really thought I was going to be using my clerical and organizational skills here."

Velma lowered her voice. "Oscar likes for people to do whatever he wants them to do. It's just the way he is. You'll get used to him."

"What if I have an ethical dilemma?" Could I really pretend not to speak English? Wasn't that lying? I hated lies.

Velma raised her eyebrows as if she had no clue what I was talking about. "An ethical dilemma?"

Did I really have to spell it out for her? Based on the clueless look in her eyes, yes, I did. "What if I don't want to pretend to be someone I'm not? What if I don't want to trick people?"

She tilted her head, her expression turning from sadly compassionate to I-feel-sorry-for-you patronizing. "Maybe you're in the wrong line of work, sweetie. Oscar's a PI. Do you think he finds answers just being nice and sweet all the time?"

"No . . . I guess I never thought about it." I really didn't have time to think any of this through. I'd applied for the job on a whim, gotten the interview that same day, and had been hired five minutes into my talk with Oscar Driscoll.

"Sometimes in the fight for justice you have to get dirty. Maybe it's better if you discover that now before you get in too deep. I'm sure there are other jobs out there for someone who's uncomfortable with this." Velma paused and stared at me. "Are you uncomfortable with this?"

Was I? It was a great question. Initially, I'd say yes. But, deep inside, part of me wanted to break away from the role I'd been pushed into playing—the girl who was always responsible. Always above reproach. The one people could count on.

Those traits were a part of me. But following the rules had gotten me nowhere.

Fatherless. Single. Living in a place I didn't want to live. Without friends.

"I . . . I don't know yet," I finally said.

"You better figure it out pretty quickly." She glanced at her smart watch. "Now, it's my lunch break, and I've got to get out of here so I can work out. But if you have any questions for me, I'll be around."

"Have fun working out. What do you do? Zumba? Free weights?" The subject seemed safe enough, like a good distraction from life's pressing questions.

"Are you kidding? All of those classes require gym memberships. Me? I go down to Easton's."

"The sporting goods store? I didn't realize they had classes there." I thought they just sold baseball bats and jerseys, but I was still learning the area.

She full out snorted. "Oh, no, sweetie. I use the treadmills there, the ones that they have for sale. They're perfect."

I stared at her, unsure if I'd heard her correctly. She didn't laugh and say JK, like my seventeen-year-old sister sometimes did. She was serious.

Working here was going to be much more interesting than I'd anticipated.

Maybe it was just what I needed—to reboot my life and reinvent Elliot Ransom.

The question was—could I reboot my life and still stay true to myself?

I'd spent the rest of the day in the office with Velma. She'd had me fill out a folder full of forms for human resources and another weird questionnaire that even asked for my blood type, if I was double-jointed, and if I'd ever participated in a lip sync competition.

I'd also had to call my new "boss" with the police station cleaning crew and confirm that I was scheduled to work tonight. Oscar had answered the ad for me initially, claiming he ran a temp agency. He'd made up a false résumé and sent it in.

After that, Velma had explained the computer system to me, run over the details of some of Oscar's current cases, and given me a few rules to keep in mind at work.

1. Never openly doubt Oscar. His ego couldn't handle it.
2. Never be late. Oscar was the only one allowed that privilege.
3. Never wear red dresses. Oscar would think I was a seductress.
4. Never talk politics. I would regret it. Like, *really* regret it. Like stick my head in a pot of boiling water regret. Those had been Velma's words, not mine.

I was still processing everything I'd learned, feeling a bit overwhelmed and *un poco* excited.

At six o'clock, I went home to change before completing the second part of my assignment. Thankfully, my mom was working at the corner drugstore and my sister had an after-school student meeting. I'd donned some khakis and a white shirt, just as I had been instructed.

I felt ready to face the jungle—literally. This was my exploration outfit, minus the boots.

I then drove down to a local apartment complex, which was actually an old motel. The place looked like it hadn't been updated in at least four decades, and the pool with its murky green water looked more like a swamp.

Apparently, most of my temporary coworkers lived here.

Before I got out of the car, my phone rang. It was Oscar.

"*Bonjour,*" he started.

"Bonjour?"

"Just a few words of wisdom." He plowed ahead as if he didn't hear me. "Remember, it never hurts to let the cops think you're their friend." His words came out in abrupt syllables.

"What?" I had no idea what he was talking about.

"You're a pretty lady. You're bound to catch someone's eye. Use that to your advantage."

"You want me to make friends with someone—possibly a cop—just so I can use them?" I clarified.

"It sounds so harsh when you say it that way. But, yeah, that's it basically."

"But—"

"Remember, your target is Detective Dylan Hunter. He's the most incompetent cop on the face of the earth, but he could still be useful."

"I know, but how—"

"No one can know you speak English or that you work for me."

"I gathered that."

"Don't let me down. Now, *sayonara.*"

Before I could argue with him, the call ended.

Being kind to someone just so I could get something from them wasn't my thing. At all. Maybe I shouldn't even be here right now. What had I been thinking?

I should simply drive home. Forget about this. I wasn't the type of girl to give in to whims. And this was why.

My insides were in a knot, and my moral compass fraught. Was I selling my soul to the devil, just to take my life to a different level?

That settled it.

I started to crank my engine, ready to leave. Before I could, a woman waved at me from beside a rundown, light-blue van.

That must be my new boss, Rosa.

A feeling of dread washed over me as I opened my car door. It looked like I needed to see this through. Tonight, at least.

I could still stay true to myself and do this job.

I hoped.

CHAPTER THREE

y hands were sweaty as I sat in the back of the van, which smelled like cumin, lavender, and Electric Youth. Someone in this vehicle was apparently obsessed with the eighties fragrance. I only recognized it because someone had gifted some to my sister once.

It's not too late to get out of a situation that's not too great.

I could still back out of this. I could fulfill my duty by cleaning tonight, just as I'd promised, then I could turn in my resignation tomorrow.

But then I remembered my sister, Ruth. She had cystic fibrosis and desperately needed a double lung transplant.

I needed a job that would help pay for medical treatment. It was the main reason my family had come here from Yerba. Healthcare in my home country had been inferior to that in the States. Since my sister and I had dual citizenship, the decision had been a no-brainer.

Yerba was a small country located beside Peru, best known for its Festival of the Chicken—*Fiesta del Pollo*—celebration. Our national holiday was a weeklong event where people dressed like—you guessed it—chickens. We did chicken dances and had contests to see who could peck food the fastest. We covered ourselves in honey and rolled in feathers. We drank milk with berries and called it . . . never mind. But it was tasty. Then we ate chicken. Lots and lots of juicy, spicy chicken.

It might sound corny, but it had been my favorite time of year, better than even Christmas. The community had come together, differences were set aside, and celebrating was the number one priority.

My dad had been native to the country, and my mom had gone there to work as a missionary after college. The two of them had fallen in love, gotten married, and two years later I came along.

Things were going well until political unrest flared. During those times of fretting, as I heard whispers of an uprising, my dad had taught me the importance of keeping my mind busy. We'd begun coming up with rhymes. To this day, I still tried to stay focused by practicing the art.

My family left Yerba just in time. A couple weeks later, the economy had imploded and the borders had been closed. Now I couldn't go back if I wanted to.

Sergio was still there, though. We had so many unfinished conversations. Knowing that we might not ever speak again or see each other face-to-face left me without the closure I craved. We'd gone from planning our future together to living like strangers.

How did one get over that?

The women around me talked about various things, including some knockoff Spanx one of them had bought and whether or not Maria was crushing on her neighbor Alexandro. A few of them even tried to include me, but I just smiled politely instead of jumping into the conversation. My mind was too preoccupied with the task at hand.

Ten minutes later, we pulled up to the Storm River Police Station. The building didn't look like the police stations back in Yerba, which had been cement buildings with bars over the windows. This place looked like an oversized beach house with its dormers and hurricane shutters.

Then again, this whole town needed to keep up appearances if it was going to remain a playground for rich politicians.

This cleaning crew worked in the evenings when the majority of law enforcement wasn't at the station. I was instructed to be invisible while inside. They'd been hired because the language barrier offered a certain level of privacy. And since sensitive information could be left out in the open or discussed among them, discretion was priority.

But, since I secretly spoke English, eavesdropping would be easy for me.

I needed to locate Detective Hunter's desk and see if I could find any information pertaining to the case there. And, as a backup, I could snoop into his files—but Oscar would deny any plausibility if I was caught.

The thought was not comforting.

Rosa doled out instructions. The woman was matronly, and I hadn't seen her smile once. She obviously ran a tight ship. As she should.

She tossed an apron at me, and I pulled it on. I squinted when I read the words across the front. The Happy Hispanic? Really?

"¡Tú! Limpia los baños."

Rosa had just assigned me to the bathrooms. Bathrooms? That wasn't going to work, though. No way would I get close to that detective's desk if I was cleaning the bathroom.

I needed to fix this.

As the rest of the crew disappeared inside, I turned to Rosa and squirmed in front of the building, trying to think quickly. The fact of the matter was that I was a terrible liar.

Finally, I told her I couldn't breathe chemicals in confined spaces. I told her cystic fibrosis, a lung disease, ran in my family. The words were true, even though I didn't have the disease.

God, forgive me. On second thought, I didn't deserve forgiveness right now. *Help me live with myself.*

Even that request didn't seem fair for me to ask.

I held my breath as I waited for Rosa's response.

Unsmiling, Rosa narrowed her eyes and finally told me to mop the floors instead.

Perfect.

I grabbed a mop from her and pushed away my shame as I entered the station.

As I slung my mop on the floor, my gaze stopped at a poster on the bulletin board. It was an image of a faceless man—one of those outlines with a question mark where features should be.

"That's the Beltway Killer," someone said beside me.

I glanced up and saw an officer. He was on the younger side with a baby face and neat blond hair. He smiled, and I immediately knew he was an extrovert and a talker. Body Language 101.

I remembered I wasn't supposed to understand English. Instead, I smiled and nodded. "Sí."

The language barrier didn't seem to deter him. "I sure do hope we find him. He's a nasty one. Killed four women already."

Four women? It seemed like I had heard something about this guy, some murmurings around town. I tried my best to avoid watching the news, but it was hard to avoid talk of this crime.

"I never thought a serial killer would hit this area." The man shook his head as he stared at the wanted poster.

I glanced at the man's name badge.

Bradford.

Seemed like an easy enough name to remember.

I continued mopping, trying to be polite but productive.

It never hurts to let the cops think you're their friend. Oscar's words echoed in my head. It was one thing to clean this place, but it was a whole different story to use someone. I wouldn't take it that far.

"I really could use that reward," Bradford continued. "One hundred thousand. Not bad, right?"

One hundred thousand? That wasn't bad at all. I could pay for my sister's surgery with money like that.

I put the idea out of my mind. No way was I capable of tracking down a serial killer. I should really track down Sarah Vance's killer before trying to tackle a case that big.

Still, my gaze scanned the words there.

The text read: Beltway Killer. Believed to be a man in late twenties/early thirties. Caucasian. 5'10". Dark hair.

At the bottom, in large print, it read, "Tips leading to the arrest could result in 100K reward."

Forget about it, Elliot.

I shoved the idea to the back of my mind. This wasn't the time to fantasize about being a great detective. I was more of the administrative type—not a field worker. My mom and dad had always driven home that point.

When I'd wanted to be on student government, they'd convinced me to be a campaign manager instead. When I'd thought about studying law, they'd convinced me to work as chief of staff for a politician. When I'd considered traveling abroad to help those less fortunate, they'd encouraged me to volunteer for my mom's mission instead. I guess they didn't want me to be an overachiever.

Bradford's radio crackled, and the man wandered away from me.

I released my breath.

Thank goodness. He'd been making me nervous.

I glanced across an open space dotted with multiple desks —the next place I needed to clean and my target area. I couldn't help but notice that the workspaces weren't evenly arranged, and I resisted the urge to nudge the desks into proper, symmetrical areas.

Things like this drove me crazy. What else drove me crazy? Pictures that were crooked. Flowers that weren't planted evenly apart. Couches that weren't parallel with the wall.

My dad had called it spatial intelligence. Said I had an excellent eye for detail. He'd encouraged me to use those traits behind the scenes to help keep less organized people in line.

I glanced around again. Only two people sat in their work areas right now. I assumed the majority of detectives worked the day shift. Of those who *were* working right now, no doubt most were on the streets instead of behind their desks.

I continued to drag my mop along the vinyl floor. As I did, I scanned the different nameplates. There was only one that I needed to find.

A quiver of anxiety rushed through me. Or was that excitement? Maybe it was both.

There had to be at least twenty desks in here. It would take a while to find what I was looking for.

I'd already scanned eight of them. I hadn't seen the detective's name.

Two men occupied the desks on the other side of the

room. It would be trickier to find anything there. But I would try.

Blend in, Elliot. Be invisible.

I continued to mop around three more desks until my eyes fell on the words I'd been waiting to read.

Dylan Hunter.

This was his desk. Finally.

I glanced around to see if anybody was watching me. One cop was on his phone, and the other stared at a computer screen. My coworkers were wiping down windows on the other side of the room. The rest of the crew must be working in the bathrooms or in the lobby area.

My heart pounded out of control as I gripped the wooden handle. Could I really do this?

I swallowed hard. My nerves were getting the best of me. Almost like this wasn't meant to be.

With a mop still in one hand, I glanced around the room again to make sure no one was watching.

They weren't.

I looked down at the desk.

The space was neat. A mug proclaiming World's Best Cup of Coffee was full of pens and pencils. A calendar lay across the middle. A computer stood guard in the corner. A picture of a man with his arm around a woman with mountains stretching behind them was taped to the monitor.

Then there was the three-tiered metal rack with files.

My heart beat even faster. One of those files could be exactly what I was looking for.

I moved my mop a few more times to make it look like I

was cleaning in case anybody saw me. As I did, my eyes scanned the words on the file tabs.

The first simply said Mackenzie. The second said Roster. Then there was the third one.

Vance.

That was it. What I was looking for. But how was I going to get that file out and open it without anyone seeing me?

I wasn't sure, but there had to be a way.

I glanced around once more. Still, no one was looking at me. I hadn't realized how invisible the cleaning crew could be. In some ways, maybe this *was* the perfect disguise to get information.

Maybe if I could just grab that file and pull it out onto the desk. I could open it and look inside to see exactly what kind of dirt this detective—the incompetent one, as Oscar had said —had dug up on our client.

But as I reached for the file, I heard a footstep behind me.

I froze, knowing I'd been caught red-handed.

CHAPTER FOUR

$\mathcal{I}$ grabbed the mop with both of my hands and twirled around.

To my surprise, a startlingly handsome man stared back at me.

He wore a blue shirt with the sleeves rolled up to his elbows. His eyes matched the shirt and were framed by thick lashes. His hair was dark blond, thick, and combed away from his face. He reminded me a touch of that actor who'd played Captain America. I didn't know his name, but my sister had been swooning over him a few weeks ago.

I went back to his eyes again. Not only was the coloring startling, but so was the depth I saw there. They seemed to penetrate into me even though the man didn't say a word.

At least he didn't say a word . . . initially.

"Can I help you?" He stared at me.

"Hola, señor," I started before spouting off more in rapid-fire Spanish.

You scared me to death. I didn't even hear you coming.

He shifted. "What? Uh . . . Que?"

Don't blow it. You're part American but don't show it. Otherwise, the detective will know it.

I licked my lips and prayed that understanding hadn't lit in my gaze. "No . . . speak . . . *inglés.*"

He squinted in confusion before nodding. He motioned to the area beside him.

"If you don't mind, work over there." He pointed to indicate where I should go—far away from his desk.

Smart man.

I stared at him another moment, not because I didn't understand what he was saying, but because he was so incredibly handsome.

"Clean?" I moved the mop to demonstrate. "There?"

He nodded slowly. "Sí. Thank you. *Gracias.*"

My heart pounded out of control as I moved away from his desk.

I had been close. So, so close to finding out that information.

And so close to being caught.

Oscar was not going to be happy. But I had done my best, especially considering I was untrained, reluctant, and slightly offended to be thrust into this position because of my skin color. Despite those things, a surge of satisfaction rose in me.

For the first time in a long time, I felt strangely alive.

I glanced back at Detective Hunter. He'd settled at his

desk and pulled out a file. It appeared he'd probably be there for the rest of the night.

As he glanced back at me, I quickly looked away.

Maybe I would have better luck next time.

If there was a next time.

I didn't finish with my cleaning job until after midnight. And I was exhausted.

Before this, I'd been employed by a large corporation where I sat in a five-story office building in a little cubicle and answered phone calls all day. It was a twenty-minute drive from my house—on a good day.

I'd only worked there two months. Misery was the word best to describe it. The pay had been okay, but I'd hated it so I'd had to weigh my options.

When I saw the job opening for Driscoll and Associates, I had applied.

Now here I was.

As I climbed into my car and drove away, I realized that I hadn't felt this energized in a very long time. Which made no sense. I was a rule follower. An administrator. A behind-the-scenes person.

In a world where people liked to be in the spotlight, I was meant to be in the background, reading books, organizing things, and making other people look good.

So why had going undercover felt so invigorating?

I wasn't sure.

I drove away from the apartment complex and headed back toward my house.

My mom wanted to stay close to DC because that's where the best medical care was for my sister. However, the prices of living away from DC were much easier to handle. Since we were near the water, the salt air also helped my sister's breathing.

I, for one, missed my home country. I missed their tasty bananas. The fresh papayas. Their rich coffee. The sunshine. The fresh air.

The community.

The Festival of the Chicken.

Sergio.

Only two blocks from home, my car sputtered.

I squeezed my eyes shut. Not again.

I knew what was coming. Smoke drifted from the hood again. My car lurched and jerked.

And then the engine died.

Thankfully, I was able to pull over to the side of the road first.

I climbed out and popped the hood. All the components blended together as I stared at the engine and various tubes.

The man who'd helped me earlier today had made the repair look so easy. But looking at all the mechanisms inside my car, I had no idea how to fix this. As soon as I got home, I was going to have to Google some tips and hope that I found some answers. I couldn't afford to pay a mechanic.

I let out a long breath and glanced down the dark sidewalk stretching in front of me. There were cracks there—and plenty of them. Grass sprang up from brokenness. Potholes littered the road, and weathered fences lined most of the area.

It wouldn't be that bad to walk home, even if it was pitch-black outside.

Right?

Our home was eight blocks away from the quaint downtown area along the river. The neighborhood where my house stood had yet to be revamped like most of the other areas had been. My mom, sister, and I were renting a house, and the owner was holding out, refusing to let anyone buy the property. I'd heard he had several offers from people who wanted to flip it and revitalize the area, taking it from ordinary into prestigious.

In some ways, I was thankful. I liked this little house with its aged wood floors and years of history etched into the scrapes and nicks. But this older area with its original cottages was also where most of the so-called local riffraff in the area chose to live. It was the only affordable housing in a community taken over by the rich.

As I walked along the cracked sidewalk with my Clorox-scented hands shoved down into the pockets of my khakis, I heard something behind me and paused.

My muscles tightened as I glanced over my shoulder.

Was somebody behind me? I'd had this feeling on the way to work, right before my car broke down. Maybe I hadn't been imagining things.

I looked back.

Maybe I was hearing things.

My dad always told me I had great instincts, though. If

my dad was right, that meant that somebody was close. I needed to take that seriously.

I thought about the man who'd helped me on the side of the road today. I thought about the word he'd muttered as he walked away. *Mantente alerta.*

That was no coincidence. It couldn't be.

Was he somehow connected with my time in Yerba?

I heard the noise again. A footstep. Behind me.

My first inclination was to slow down, to see who it might be.

But I couldn't afford that luxury. If someone was behind me, I needed *to run like I'd otherwise be done.*

I quickened my steps. I wasn't ready to sprint yet. But I would, if necessary.

Another footstep sounded.

Sweat spread across my brow. Why would someone be following me?

None of the scenarios that played out in my mind were what I wanted to envision.

What if it was the Beltway Killer? I fit his victims' profile. I was a woman in my twenties.

No, why would the Beltway Killer be coming after me? I'd simply seen that poster earlier, and now my mind was playing tricks on me, making me paranoid.

As the footsteps grew closer, I knew I had to act. I had to leave. And fast.

I broke out into a run.

I spotted my house up ahead. The little one-story bungalow that I had called home for the past three months. A rusty chain-link fence surrounded it. Right now, it just seemed like another obstacle separating me from safety.

I reached the flimsy barrier and fumbled with the latch. Finally, the gate opened, and I ran up the sidewalk to my front door. I almost dropped the keys, but I caught them.

Somehow, I unlocked my door. As soon as I was inside, I slammed it shut and hit all the locks. Then I peered out the window.

The shadow was there.

On the edge of the property.

I couldn't see a face. All I could see was a hazy image.

Someone *had* been following me. I had no doubt about that.

But as quickly as I'd seen him, he disappeared. He walked away.

I released my breath.

Until I heard a footstep behind me.

CHAPTER FIVE

"Elliot? What are you doing?"

I twirled around and saw my mother standing there, pulling her house robe closer around her. She'd obviously been trying to sleep. I say *trying* because I knew she never fully went to sleep until both of her daughters were home—we were all adjusting to life without Dad. Life on our own.

"My car broke down so I had to walk the rest of the way home," I quickly explained.

My mom's eyebrows shoved together. She looked younger than her fifty-two years and had been mistaken for my older sister on more than one occasion. I'd inherited my boyish figure from her, but my dark hair was from my dad.

Mom had light honey-blonde hair that she usually kept pulled back in a ponytail. The fine lines on her face hadn't appeared until two months ago when my father had been taken away entirely too soon.

We'd just moved here, and Dad had gotten a job as maintenance manager for a nearby resort. One day, while he'd been at work, he'd had a heart attack. By the time the ambulance had arrived, it was too late. He was gone.

And the rest of us were forced to go on without him in this strange new place.

"I'm sorry to hear that about your car," my mom said. "But why are you acting so strange?"

"Because acting strange is a lot more fun than acting normal?" I tried to blow off her question so she wouldn't be worried. She had enough on her mind trying to take care of my sister.

But worry was my mother's middle name.

"I had no idea that this new job you're working would keep you out so late." Her voice scooped lower with suspicion.

"Sorry, Mama. But it will require some overtime hours. I'm okay with that because I get paid extra."

She shook her head. "It's just too bad you can't find another good government job. At least working for the law firm is a respectable job."

My face grew paler. My mom didn't know the truth. She thought Driscoll and Associates was a law practice, and I hadn't corrected her. Guilt haunted me at the thought.

I knew I needed to tell her the truth, but Mama was so proud of me. If she found out I was secretly working for a private investigator . . . she wouldn't feel the same way.

She would equate PI work with danger.

She leaned toward me and sniffed. "Why do you smell like cleaner?"

I tried to keep my expression even. "Cleaner? I . . . it's part of my job duties. I'm the low person on the totem pole, as the expression goes. That means I get stuck cleaning up."

She let out an unapproving grunt. "I see."

"How is Ruth?" I deposited my purse on the table and glanced out the window again. Whoever had been following me appeared to be gone.

"She had a good day. No complaints." My mom wiped her hand across the dining room table, as if checking for dust. Our house was simple, but my mom insisted it remain clean.

Perhaps I'd gotten some of my OCD qualities from her.

"She wore her vest without giving you a hard time?" My sister had to wear a device twice a day that helped to keep her lungs clear. The vest vibrated, loosening up the mucus in her lungs to help prevent cystic fibrosis flare-ups.

"She sure did."

"That's something to be thankful for."

My mom frowned. "I fear she's going to need that lung transplant sooner rather than later though. Her lungs are getting worse."

Sadness pressed on me at her words. I knew my mom was worried about my sister. I was worried about her too, for that matter. But I tried not to show it. I tried to be strong for my mom. She'd been through so much over the past few months.

"When it comes time, we're going to have the money. It's

going to be just fine. God will provide." She raised her praise hands. My mom was such a person of faith.

"I know He will."

Her face fell. "I'm sorry you have to see my lack of faith sometimes. I've always taught you to trust God, yet I fret about things way too often. Especially now that your father . . ."

"It's been a tough couple months. Cut yourself some slack." I pulled my mom into a quick hug.

She nodded and stepped back, but I saw the tears in her eyes. Thankfully she was making some good friends at the church we'd begun to attend. She needed people to lean on, people outside the family. We were all carrying the same grief.

"Go get some rest," my mom said.

I nodded and stepped back.

Sleep sounded great. I had a long day tomorrow. I needed to go into the office during the day, and I'd need to work for the cleaning agency in the evening.

A surprising sense of excitement rushed through me. For the first time in a long time, I was looking forward to my job.

In my room, I lay in my bed and tried to sleep but couldn't. I had too much on my mind.

I'd figured today would discourage me from moving forward with my new job. But a part of me felt more alive than I had in a long time. Could I really see myself doing this for the long haul?

I would do whatever was best for my sister.

Health insurance had been a real struggle. Since no one in my family had a job that offered it, we were paying out of pocket. But those premiums seemed astronomical, and the deductibles sucked any extra money that we already had.

I reached over to my nightstand and grabbed the wooden jewelry box my father had given me only a week before he died. The piece was beautiful and made from rich mahogany, with various drawers and two sides that pulled out to hang necklaces on.

The gift had seemed slightly strange since I didn't wear much jewelry. But my dad had probably figured I could use this for the rest of my life.

I ran my hand over the top of it and closed my eyes. I missed my dad so much. I loved my mom. I really did. But my dad had been the one I'd felt the soul connection with. He was the one who understood me.

Not only had I lost my community, but I also lost my biggest supporter when my father had passed away.

I placed the jewelry box back on my nightstand and pushed away my tears. Instead, my mind drifted through all the new people I'd met today, starting with the man who'd stopped to help me on the side of the road.

He was typical of the weekenders in the area, with his fancy suit and flashy car. He'd said *mantente alerta.* Stay alert. Could I have misheard? Maybe he'd muttered, "Maintain to it later" or "Maybe I'll see you later."

I had no idea. Was I reading too much into something that wasn't valid?

And there was Oscar. He was a character within himself. I didn't quite know what to do with him nor did I really trust him.

Then there had been Velma. Was she someone who could be a friend one day? She was probably only a few years older than I, but my scruples seemed to perplex her.

What about that feeling I'd had earlier—that I was being followed? Was it an overactive imagination? Or had someone really been behind me? And, if that was the case, why?

An uneasy feeling sloshed inside me. As it did, I twisted my hair back into a bun and scooted down farther in bed. I needed to sleep. I needed to stop thinking and turn my brain off for a little while.

But it was going to be easier said than done.

Instead, I tried to rhyme.

There once was a girl with a bun. She thought she could take a run. But the lies that chased after seemed to come faster, until she realized she was done.

CHAPTER SIX

The next morning, I had to take the bus to work. It wasn't ideal, but I was thankful that I *had* a bus I could take. Though I'd looked up some videos online about how to fix my car, I'd run out of time to actually do it.

Velma smiled at me from her desk when I walked in. "I brought in some muffins. Help yourself." She nudged the plastic container toward me.

"That was nice of you. Thank you." I took one of the blueberry pastries and walked into my office. As I sat at my desk, somebody else walked in behind me.

It was a guy probably a few years older than I was, with short dark hair, loose clothing, and a T-shirt that proclaimed, "Birds aren't real." He wore skater shoes and a backward baseball cap. Tattoos peeked out from beneath his sleeves, his shirt collar, and even stretched across his hands. The faint outline of a mustache and beard graced the edges of his face.

"You must be the new girl." He shuffled toward his desk at a quick pace. "I'm Michael Straley, Oscar's other assistant."

"I'm Elliot. Nice to meet you." I reached my hand forward, and we shook.

He took a seat at the desk next to me and nodded at my muffin. "I wouldn't eat that, by the way."

"Why not? Velma brought it in."

He lowered his voice. "If she ever brings food, politely decline. If you've ever thought about becoming gluten-free, now is the time. And that's a true fact."

He picked up some apples from a pile of snacks on his desk—a pile that included two granola bars, pretzels, and a pack of gum. He juggled the Granny Smiths a minute before tossing me one.

I caught it and placed it on the desk in front of me, still totally confused. Even though fruit was my comfort food, truth be told, I wanted the muffin right now. My palette had started to anticipate it already.

"I still don't understand." I lifted the treat, ready to take a bite. I loved gluten and everything it stood for.

He lowered his voice. "She probably got it while she was dumpster diving."

I wanted to barf up the muffin even though I hadn't taken a bite yet. "The trash?"

Michael gave me a look that was nothing short of amused. He took a bite of his apple and leaned back.

"Are you for real?" I clarified.

"Velma is the cheapest person I know. She splits her two-ply toilet paper to make it into one ply. She washes paper towels, dries them, and then uses them again. It's better if you know these things now."

"Was that why she went to Easton's Sporting Goods to work out yesterday?"

Michael pointed at me and clicked his tongue. "Bingo! I can see that I'm going to need to show you the ropes around here. Speaking of which, how did it go last night?"

"Not great—" Before I could finish explaining, the door to Oscar's office flew open. His massive figure stood there, and his beady eyes were like laser beams that burned into my very soul.

"Elliot. In my office. Now."

For the first time in a very long time, I felt like I was being called in to see the principal.

And I didn't like it.

My hands were sweaty as I lowered myself into the fake leather chair across from Oscar.

"Good morning," I started, trying to put my best foot forward.

He continued to stare at me, no trace of a smile in sight. "How did it go last night, *Signora*?"

"That's Italian . . . never mind." I shook my head. "Last night? Do you mean, at the police station?"

I was buying myself some time to formulate an answer, and I hadn't expected to feel this intimidated by the man, but I did.

"Yes, of course at the police station. What do you think I'm talking about? A blind date you went on?" His cheeks turned red as he stared at me, his face nearly vibrating with emotion.

I raised my eyebrows but tried to keep my expression otherwise placid. "Well, I did manage to get into the station, and I did manage to clean. I did not, however, manage to find any information out on Flash Slivinski."

Oscar's hand slammed into the desk. "I sent you there for one reason and one reason only. This isn't a very good start to your job, Dora."

Dora? What? Had he forgotten my name in these brief few minutes?

Sweat formed across my brow. "It wasn't all my fault—"

"No excuses."

"But—" I needed to tell him that the detective had been there. Then it would make sense why I hadn't gotten the information.

"Failure is not an option here. I gave you a job to do. You are officially on notice. If you are not successful, then you're out of here. *Capisce*?"

I stared at him, certain that I didn't understand. He couldn't fire me after one day. He hadn't even heard my explanation. "No. No capisce."

He sighed and glowered at me. "Listen, Dora. I like you. I want you to succeed. Let me give you a few tips . . ."

"Okay," I said, probably a little too quickly. Now wasn't the time to correct my name.

"There's an art to what I do."

"An art? Well, I'm a quick learner—"

"Starting with this. Whenever you eavesdrop, you can't let people know. Become invisible. It's why I hired you. You represent the plight of the undocumented worker."

"But I'm not undocumented—"

"Sure you are, non-gringa."

"No, I'm really not—"

"You're out there, speaking another language. No one thinks anything about you. They have more important people to deal with."

"But I mostly speak English. And I'm a US citizen—"

"Now get outta here." Oscar pointed his thick finger toward the door. "Michael has your job for today. He'll help show you the ropes. *Hasta la vista*, baby!"

Before I could even stand from my seat to leave, Oscar turned the TV on, propped his feet up on the desk, and started watching a soap opera.

Exactly what kind of job had I taken? I didn't know.

But I needed to quickly figure out if I was going to see this assignment through or not.

Because if I couldn't respect my boss, could I really work for him?

Before I could walk back to my desk, Michael met me at the door and nodded toward the exit. "You and I are out of here."

I sucked in a breath, trying to understand what he meant.

My mind, of course, went to worst-case scenarios. "What do you mean? Did you just get fired too?"

"Oscar fired you?" Michael's eyes widened with surprise.

I shook my head, realizing I might be overreacting. "He didn't exactly fire me. He just threatened to."

"Oh." Michael seemed to relax as he waved a hand in the air. "Get used to it. He'll say that a lot. That's a true fact."

Suddenly, I was having second thoughts about working here. I liked stability. It was more than just liking stability, I *needed* stability. I needed a steady paycheck.

"So when I said you and I are out of here, I meant that you and I are going to trace Flash Slivinski's steps on the day before the murder occurred. We're going to be out of the office today. You okay with that?"

Getting away from Oscar sounded like a great idea.

I hurried back into the office and plucked my purse from the desk I'd hardly had time to get acquainted with yet. "Let's go."

A few minutes later, we climbed into Michael's old minivan. And when I said old, I didn't mean charmingly old. I meant, it was probably fifteen years past its prime, needed a new paint job, and screamed, "I have no social status."

The inside smelled like fast food. A dirty sock was strewn in the back seat, and mail had been shoved between the front seats. I desperately wanted to clean the van for him, but that would be overstepping, especially considering we'd just met.

"So, where exactly are we going to start with this?" I rubbed my hands on my jeans, still unsure how I felt about everything.

"We're going to start by heading to Flash's condo. We're going to look at things there."

"Interesting."

"You ever done this before?"

Only if cleaning my dead Aunt Marie's house counted. "Never."

"I'll teach you the ropes."

"Great. I'm a fast learner."

He smiled, but something about the action almost seemed skeptical. I ignored it. I hated when people underestimated me.

Instead, I drew in a deep breath. "So, has Oscar had a lot of other assistants before me?"

Michael's eyebrows shot up before he quickly leveled his expression. "You heard?"

"Maybe."

He shrugged, almost as if hesitant to answer. "He goes through assistants like some people go through toilet paper."

"That's not comforting. Why is that?" I felt more of my stability slipping away.

"He starts people off with high pay to lure them in," Michael said. "But Oscar also realizes they'll only last a maximum of two days, so he's not really losing that much money through his process."

"Why do people last such a short period of time?" Suddenly, this was all seeming like a bad idea. And that truly was a true fact, as Michael seemed prone to say.

Michael shrugged again. "Oscar can be . . . difficult. But I'll let you see for yourself."

I didn't need to see for myself. I'd already experienced it. The man was rude, insulting, demanding, and unforgiving. Why was I still working for him?

"How long did his last assistant last?" I asked out of curiosity.

"Three hours."

My eyes widened. It was worse than I thought. "What happened?"

"Oscar . . . told her she was going to have to crawl under a house to look for evidence a sewage line had been tampered with. It was for an insurance case."

"That doesn't sound like fun."

"Especially not since she was claustrophobic."

Meanwhile, was Oscar watching TV and doing interviews?

I stared out the window, trying to calm my nerves. "So, it sounds like you do things like this a lot—the footwork for investigations. What about Oscar's associates? He's not the only PI at the firm, is he?"

"He named the business that when he was the only employee. He thought people would take it more seriously if he added 'associates.' I suppose, practically speaking, that I'm an associate, though Oscar would never admit that. I do the footwork with almost every case we work." Michael shrugged and glanced at me, a look of almost amusement in his gaze.

Exactly what kind of job had I taken? I'd been so anxious to find something new.

But what if I'd just made a huge mistake?

CHAPTER SEVEN

Twenty minutes later, Michael and I pulled up to a ten-story condo complex on the outskirts of DC. Michael grabbed some keys from his pocket as we hurried up the sidewalk toward the front door. As he led me into the building, he looked like he had done stuff like this a million times before.

"So, you know anything about Flash?" As Michael crossed his arms, a thorny tattoo peeked out on his muscular bicep.

We paused at the elevator. "Only that he supposedly killed a woman and that he's some kind of famous golfer."

"Some kind of famous golfer?" Michael chuckled and pressed the button for the top floor. "He is one of the most famous golfers in the world."

"I guess my family really isn't big on keeping up with stuff like that. I find pop culture to be a waste of time." We stepped into the elevator.

"I just thought everybody knew who he was. His name has been all over TV." Michael glanced at me, utter shock lighting his gaze.

"I actually only moved to this country a few months ago, and my family doesn't have a TV. My mom considers it a royal waste of time." I waited for his reaction. People in the US never seemed to understand that sentiment. "My mom often says that we pity people in other countries because of what they don't have, but she pities people in the US because we have so much yet we have so little joy."

"Sounds wise." Michael gave me a second glance as we stepped off the elevator. "Where are you from?"

"Yerba."

"Yerba? I've heard of it. There was some kind of political unrest there recently."

My stomach clenched as he said the words. "That's right. That's where I'm from."

"Yet now you're here."

"Thankfully, my family was able to get out when we did. I have dual citizenship, so here we are."

"Sounds dope."

"Isn't that a drug?"

"It is but—" He shook his head. "Never mind. It's also an expression."

I still had so much to learn about American culture.

Michael slipped a key into the door and pushed it open. A moment later, Flash's condo stared at us.

The place was beautiful.

A wall of windows lined the outside of the living quarters.

The furnishings were ultra-modern and sleek. The whole place smelled like expensive leather. No expense had been spared.

Yet everything seemed impersonal, almost like it could be a hotel room. There were no pictures or anything that gave it a homey feel. At least, not here in the living area.

My breath stopped when I saw the fingerprint dust along the kitchen counter. When I spotted the blood spatter on the couch. When I noticed the missing rug beneath the coffee table—some of the blood spatter showed the edges of where it had been, a chilling reminder about what had happened here.

Nausea roiled in my stomach.

"The crime-scene cleaners can't come for a couple more days," Michael explained.

"I see." I paused, waiting to follow Michael's lead. "So what are we looking for?"

Michael pulled on some rubber gloves before tossing a pair to me. "Just pretend like you're in one of those detective shows."

"I don't watch detective shows."

"That's right. Look for anything out of the ordinary. The police have already been here. I've already been here. But we're starting from scratch. So having fresh eyes on the case will do us a lot of good."

I hoped I didn't let him down. I *hated* letting people down.

Since details were my specialty, I hoped the slightly OCD part of my personality didn't fail me now.

"Will do." I decided to start on the right side of the room and move around the edges. Then I'd work my way in.

Slowly, I paced along the walls, soaking in the artwork. Looking at the glass-top tables. Running my hands along the edge of the fireplace mantle.

Why would someone want to live in such a cold space? It made me not care for Flash—which was ridiculous. I'd never even met the man. But a person's environment reflected the inner workings of the person.

At least, they did in my humble opinion.

Back in Yerba, my room had been tidy, with rich colors and photos of my memories. Memories with my dad. With my best friend, Tahlia. With my fiancé who was no longer my fiancé.

A handmade rug from my neighbor graced my floor. A quilt my grandmother had made blanketed my bed. Growing plants added life to the space.

I wasn't saying my way was superior to another's. But this place, Flash's place, just seemed so unwelcoming.

I paused by the massive windows that looked down into the street below, with its restaurants and shops and people scurrying about.

Part of the seal around the frame was uneven, I realized.

As I reached up, I discovered a good reason for it.

A small camera had been mounted there. It would have been easy to miss. The device was only the size of a pencil eraser, and it had blended in with the seal around the window frame.

"Michael, you're going to want to see this."

I watched as Michael pulled the camera from the window and placed it in a plastic bag.

"Are you going to take that down to the police station?" I asked, trying to figure out our next move.

"Not a chance." He put the bag in his pocket.

"But couldn't you get arrested if you don't? Aren't we tampering with a crime scene?"

He pulled his hat off and then put it back on. "The police have already come and gotten everything they need from this room. Right now, our job is to prove that our client is innocent. I have no idea what's on this camera or where the information is being transmitted, but we're going to find out."

Part of me was uncomfortable with that. The right thing to do would be to turn this evidence over to the police. Then again, I didn't know how this PI gig worked. We were supposed to act in the best interest of our clients, and, if the police had cleared the crime scene and let us in, then I also supposed that this was fair game.

Right? I was navigating new and unfamiliar waters here.

I swallowed my misgivings and turned toward Michael. "What now?"

"Now we are going to continue to trace Flash's footsteps on the day the murder occurred."

"I never asked, where is Flash right now?"

"He's staying in a second home in Arlington."

"I'm surprised they let him out on bail."

"When you have money, a lot of stuff is allowed." Michael swung his keys around his finger. "You ready to go?"

"You're calling the shots. I'm just here to learn from you."

A few minutes later, we were in Michael's minivan again, and he cranked the engine. As we took off down the road, he glanced at me.

"Good job back there. How'd you see that camera?"

Before launching into my explanation, I prepared myself for his reaction. "I know this is going to sound strange, but I really like for things to be square and plumb. It's a weird quirk I have."

"Square?" He gave me another glance.

"It's called spatial intelligence. I'm pretty sure those are overstated words to say that I am a little too Type A for my own good. For example, from the moment I walk into a house, I can tell if the builder was skilled or not based on how the walls line up. If a rug isn't placed correctly on a floor or furniture isn't set up evenly, it can drive me crazy. Oh, and when someone takes a picture and the horizon is crooked in the background? I can hardly look at the photo."

"That's . . . interesting."

"Interesting is a nice word of saying strange. It's okay."

"Maybe a little strange, but not strange necessarily in a bad way. What did you do before you took this job?" His rolling voice sounded curious.

I frowned. "I worked for an insurance company. I was actually pretty good at my job. I was able to see inconsistencies in different reports that were being filed."

"Then why did you switch?" He turned down the hip-hop music blaring through the speakers.

"I pretty much hated it. Plus, the commute was a minimum of twenty minutes but more often closer to forty. Spending that much time in my vehicle isn't the way I want to live my best life, if you know what I mean."

"Yeah, I get that. The commute into DC is horrendous, and that's on a good day."

I shifted, glancing at him again and wondering how much I should share. He was a good listener and he seemed interested. He had a bit of a boy next door vibe, only a little edgier.

"Before that, I worked a government job," I said.

He raised his eyebrows. "Was it in building inspections?"

I couldn't resist a smile. "No, not exactly. I was actually chief of staff for a legislator in the province where I lived."

Surprise lit his eyes. "Going from chief of staff for a politician to working as a sidekick for Oscar? Girl, what were you thinking? That's like going from a fine filet mignon to a ninety-nine-cent greasy burger special."

"I know the shift seems weird. I'm twenty-seven, and I should have things figured out by now. But I don't. Sometimes circumstances that are beyond your control dictate the trajectory of your life. I've just learned that I have to be okay with that. At least for now."

He turned off the highway. "If you could be doing anything that you wanted to do what would it be?"

I blanched, surprised at his inquiry. People never asked

me that. They seemed to always tell me what I should be doing instead.

"Truthfully, I've always liked just having a simple life. I never wanted to be married to my career. I wanted to allow room in my life to breathe. To get to know neighbors. To take care of family. To better myself by reading books, to be involved in church and help others. I don't buy into the notion that my whole life needs to revolve around my work or that I need to find value in myself based on how busy I am."

"Deep," Michael muttered.

I glanced at him, trying to read the meaning behind his words. "I take it you don't agree."

"Actually, I do agree. I do think there's more to life than getting in your hours from nine to five. Or from seven to six, which is more like it on most days. It's the rat race, and it's not always where I want to be. But I have bills to pay, and that dictates how I spend my days. True fact."

"My mom was always really great about encouraging me not to go into debt so I could have more freedom in life. Be a slave to no one and nothing. That's what she taught me."

"And did that work?"

"It did, but then circumstances changed." I stopped before I said too much.

I really didn't want to get into my father's death and how the life insurance policy we thought he had he didn't actually have. He had been the sole breadwinner for my mom and sister. Back in Yerba, I'd had my own place and made my own money. But when we decided to come back to the States, things changed.

Michael pulled to a stop in front of a restaurant near the edge of town and on the outskirts of a golf course. But as he put his van back into Park, he didn't make a move to get out. "Spatial intelligence, huh? I'm fascinated. In fact, I'm still thinking about it."

"It's really not that exciting." I blushed. I did that when I talked about myself too much.

"Are you like Monk? Does it drive you crazy when things are out of order?" He waggled his fingers in the air to drive home some kind of point.

"First of all, I actually don't know who Monk is. And, secondly, I notice things, but I don't obsess about them. Life is just too short for that."

He turned toward me, his hazel eyes sparkling. "How about me? Am I symmetrical?"

I felt my cheeks heat even more as I glanced at him. But I didn't need to study him to know that answer. I'd noticed those details as soon as we'd first met.

"Most people aren't," I started, rubbing my throat. "That's why people's glasses never quite fit like they should and need to be adjusted. That's why people say they have a good side and a bad side."

"So you didn't answer my question." Michael continued to stare at me, a boyish, almost mischievous look in his eyes.

After a moment of hesitation I finally said, "Your left eye is larger than your right, as is your eyebrow—but only slightly. Also, one ear is higher than the other, and the left side of your beard is a little thicker than the right side."

I cleared my throat and looked away, feeling like I was probably being too honest. People said that's what they wanted, but it really wasn't. What people really wanted was affirmation usually.

"You know, I've always thought my face was a little strange. Now you confirmed it." He rubbed his jaw.

Guilt flooded me. "I didn't mean—"

"It's okay." Michael nudged me with his elbow. "I like imperfect things. Now, you ready to work Flash 'the Birdie' Slivinski's case?"

"One question first. Is this guy's middle name really Birdie?" That had confused me since the first time I heard it. I felt certain I was missing something.

"No. Birdie is a golf term."

That made sense. I nodded. "I see."

"And it's a nickname that was given to the man because he's a consummate jerk." Michael shrugged. "Now, you ready?"

I let out my breath and nodded. "Ready as I'll ever be."

"Okay. Let's go."

As we stepped out, I reminded myself that I was so much better with numbers and schedules than I was people. I had a feeling that was going to be a problem.

CHAPTER EIGHT

A few minutes later, we were inside the Green Leaf
Tavern, a bar disguised as a restaurant. The insides
were dim and felt a little more cave-like than I preferred. The
tables weren't evenly spaced out, but I knew that was a detail
that only someone like me cared about.

Even though it was lunchtime, the establishment was only
about a third full. Sports memorabilia decorated the walls,
eighties rock played overhead, and the whole place smelled
like yeast.

Alcohol, I supposed.

I found the scent appalling. However, the decaying scent
of leaves in the jungle made me feel right at home, so I wasn't
exactly normal.

We headed toward the only employee I saw—the
bartender. The man was tall and trendy with a neat beard and

oversized glasses. He was drying a glass and placing it back on a rack when we walked up.

I wondered how Michael did in these situations. Could he stay focused? Or was he all over the place? I was still trying to gauge whether or not my initial assessment was correct.

"What can I get you guys?"

"I'll just have a Coke." Michael straddled the bar stool.

"Nothing for me," I said, sitting beside him.

The guy grabbed a glass, put it under a dispenser beneath the counter, and handed it to Michael. I tried to look like I belonged here, but it totally wasn't my scene. I felt more like a spider monkey that had gotten loose in the inner city.

"Do I know you?" The bartender eyed Michael for a minute.

Michael's shoulders tightened ever-so-slightly. The question had made him uncomfortable. But why?

"Nah, man. I've never been in here before."

The bartender squinted, as if he didn't believe him.

"We're hoping you might be able to help us out," Michael started, aptly changing the subject. His voice changed back to friendly and conversational, like he could be someone's best friend. I made a mental note of that, but I'd have to figure that out later.

I observed the bartender, starting with the name on his shirt—Zack. The man picked up another glass and began to dry it. Was this his nervous tic?

I thought it was a good guess. Either that, or he was really dedicated to his job.

"What do you need to know?" Zack asked.

"We're trying to find out some information about Flash Slivinski." Michael leaned his arms on the counter, looking like they were two old friends catching up. "We heard he came in here the day of the murder."

"Maybe he did, maybe he didn't. Are you reporters?"

"We're actually private investigators that Flash hired," Michael said. "We're trying to retrace his steps so we can prove his innocence."

Something seemed to change in the man's gaze. "I did see Flash in here that day."

"Was he acting like himself?" Michael began flipping a packet of sweetener.

There it was. The ADHD. The need to always move.

The man was clearly my opposite. Where I was focused, neat, and quiet, Michael was all over the place, messy, and outgoing.

"From what I heard, Flash was a regular here," Michael continued.

"Yes, he was a frequent patron." Zack pointed to the wall in the distance. "He even gave us some of his memorabilia to display."

I glanced to where he pointed and saw some signed photos on the wall. I'd noticed them when I walked in, but I just assumed the owner was a big golf fan.

"Flash was shooting the breeze with some of our regulars. I'd say he stayed here for a good three hours. The last thirty minutes or so Flash was here, that woman came in."

"By that woman, do you mean Sarah Vance, the woman

who died?" Michael clarified, still flipping the packet of sugar.

I watched the bartender's expression, trying to pick up on any hidden clues. Not that I was an expert. But, in general, I considered myself a pretty good judge of character.

Zack's gaze shifted back and forth, as if he was processing the conversation and formulating his answers.

Finally, he nodded. "That's right. Sarah."

"Had you ever seen her in here before?" Michael asked.

"No. I had the impression that maybe she was in DC on a work trip." He shrugged. "Something about her gave off that vibe. She wore a business suit, and her purse looked more like a briefcase."

"When did the two of them start talking?" Michael finally put the packet down and took a sip of his soda.

"She ended up sitting beside Flash at the bar, and they struck up a conversation. They seemed to get along really well. They talked and laughed and talked and laughed some more. Then they both got up to leave at the same time. And that was that."

Michael nodded slowly. "So it appeared they were on good terms when they left?"

"They seemed to be on very good terms." The way Zack said "good terms" was filled with suggestion.

"I'm assuming you told the police this also?" Michael asked, taking another sip of his drink.

"Yeah. I'm not sure how it helps the investigation. I can only assume that they went back to his place, had some type of disagreement, and she ended up dead. It really is a shame.

I've always liked Flash. Can't really see him doing anything like that. Someone who's that great of a golfer can't be a scum in other areas of his life, right?"

That remained to be seen.

Michael leaned closer. "You didn't, by chance, see anybody leave directly after they did? Maybe somebody who followed them out?"

The bartender paused from his neurotic drying of the glasses. "Now that you mention it, someone else did leave probably three or four minutes after Flash did. I didn't think anything of it."

A spark appeared in Michael's gaze. "Do you have a name for this person?"

"I don't, but I can find out."

"If you would do that for us, we'd be grateful."

The bartender leveled his gaze. "I won't do it for you, but I'll do it because I like Flash. Give me a second."

I watched as the man sorted through some receipts. A moment later, he held up one. "The man's name was Art Smith. That's all I know about him. If you want any more information, you're going to have to find him yourself."

"What now?" I asked once Michael and I were back in the minivan. A strange thrill of excitement zinged through my blood. "Are we going to go chase down this Art guy?"

Michael glanced at the time on his console. "Unfortunately, not now. We need to head back, especially if you have to report to the cleaning service this evening."

I bit back my disappointment. I'd forgotten about that. "You're right."

"We do have just enough time to grab a bite to eat, though. How about if we get a late lunch?"

"Some lunch sounds great." I really shouldn't spend the extra money, and I had packed a lunch, complete with a peanut butter sandwich and apple. But by the time I got back to the office to eat, I was going to be famished.

Michael pulled up to the harbor area in Storm River. This part of town was located on the edge of the tourist area, part of the original infrastructure of the area. It had a more raw feel than the polished retail area.

I didn't come down here very often. I tried not to spend any money on things that were unnecessary—including eating out and most entertainment. It wasn't that I was frugal or a saint. It was simply that money was tight.

But this area was, by far, my favorite over the other areas in town. Several seafood restaurants were right on the water where boats docked out front. A couple small stores were also located in the space and parking lots backed up to the area.

We climbed out, and Michael led me toward a building in the distance with a sign above it proclaiming The Board Room. I'd never heard of it before.

Several people called out hello to Michael as he entered. He appeared to be a regular.

We were able to be seated immediately at a table by the window overlooking the water. Bean bags slouched in the corner, shelves full of games lined the side walls, and oversized Scrabble tiles decorated the space in between.

"It's a board game café," Michael explained. "Who needs a plain old coffee shop when, instead, you can play Settlers of Catan for hours while drinking and eating?"

I loved board games. I especially loved ones that made you think and strategize. I already knew I was going to love it here.

"This is great," I murmured.

Michael smiled. "It's my favorite. Plus, I like supporting local businesses."

"By the way, I've been meaning to ask about your shirt." I pointed to the "Birds Aren't Real" text across his chest. "Is that a joke?"

"Birds are a government conspiracy. They're actually robotic, flying spies."

I stared at him, trying to interpret whether or not he was serious. He didn't laugh.

Before we could talk anymore, Michael's phone rang.

He glanced at the screen before excusing himself and answering. "Hey there! How's my girl?"

His girl? No doubt Michael had a girlfriend. He seemed like the fun-loving kind of guy who'd turn a lot of heads. I also felt like he had stories buried deep inside him—stories I was anxious to hear.

I tried to tune out their conversation by glancing around, but I was unsuccessful.

"I know," Michael continued. "I can't wait to see you later

either. I love you, and thanks for calling, sweetie. I'll see you at home."

Something about the way he said the words caused a flash of jealousy in me. It was ridiculous, really. It wasn't that I wanted to hear Michael talk to me like that. But it would be nice to have *someone* who might talk to me like that.

My fiancé . . . well, to say the least, he'd been a bust. We'd talked about running off and starting a life together. Forgetting about a big wedding. Forgetting custom and tradition.

Then, one day, he'd ghosted me. It was almost like he disappeared off the face of the earth never to be seen again. After twenty-four hours of him ignoring my phone calls, I got a text stating that he'd had a great awakening and realized we'd never work.

Cold feet? Maybe.

All I knew was that it had hurt. Sometimes, it still did.

"Sorry about that." Michael put his phone on the table and turned back to me.

"It's no problem."

Without missing a beat, he picked up his menu. "So, aside from board games, this place is also known for their charcuterie boards. They have all kinds."

"Sounds interesting."

"My favorite, especially at lunch time, is the hot dog board. It comes with every topping you could want, two different kinds of chips, fruit, and macaroni salad. Interested in splitting something?"

"Now I am." I just hoped it wasn't too expensive. I was definitely on a budget.

"Great. And, by the way, this is on Oscar," Michael said, as if reading my mind. "We are on the clock."

"Really?" I wasn't used to my employers paying for my lunches.

"Yeah, of course. Just like he's paying for my gas. Oscar makes enough money that he can afford to do this. Especially considering that he doesn't really do anything."

I shifted in my seat. "That's the second time you've alluded to that. What do you mean he doesn't do anything? He was esteemed after solving the Ernesto case."

"All he does is bark out orders and fund the operations—and that is a big part of it. I'm not saying the man isn't brilliant. Or maybe I should say that he *was*, at one time in his life, brilliant. But now, all he does is drink most of the day, leer at women, and watch TV. He's pretty much good for nothing."

Michael's words did something strange to my heart. I'd been wanting to work with the best. And it turned out I was working for a louse instead? I didn't even know what to say. I needed to figure out what was important to me before I invested too much into this job.

The waitress came, and we ordered. Then Michael grabbed Jenga from the shelf and set it on the table. "Until our food gets here."

"Sounds fun." I hadn't played in years.

He pulled the first wooden block out from the tower. "Your turn."

I played it safe and grabbed an outer piece from the middle. The uneven edges drove me crazy, but I choose to ignore it. I would have totally straightened them before we started, but I didn't know Michael well enough and didn't want to seem too psycho.

Michael turned to me as he made his next play. He flipped an extra Jenga piece in the air.

This man needed a fidget spinner. Yes, the device had even made its way down to Yerba.

"So, Elliot, huh? That's a unique name for a girl. What's the story behind it?"

It wasn't often that people asked me that question, but it just so happened to be one of my favorite stories to tell.

"Actually, my mom was a missionary from the United States to Yerba. Her favorite author was someone named Elisabeth Elliot. She actually named me after her."

Michael stared at me, an unreadable expression in his eyes. "Elisabeth Elliot was a missionary too, right?"

My eyebrows shot up. "Yes, that's correct. Not many people know that."

"Not many people know this either, but I actually went to a Christian high school. I've read her books before."

Surprise washed through me. As I glanced down, I saw that one of the tattoos on Michael's finger was a cross with the word "Jesus" on either side. Now it made more sense.

My curiosity grew. "If you don't mind me asking, how did you end up working for Oscar?"

Michael shrugged and leaned back. "I needed a stable job. He hired me initially so I could run background checks and stuff on the computer. But as he's started to do less and less on his cases, he's been assigning me to do more and more.

That's why I'm hoping he'll actually hire someone who's going to last for more than two days. I can't do it all."

"I take it you like working for him. I mean, you haven't quit." I watched his reaction carefully so I wouldn't miss the truth.

Michael shrugged again. "I love investigating and finding the bad guys. This pays better than I would be getting paid at the police station. I don't really want to work for the government up in DC. So this works for now. Plus, it keeps me close to Chloe."

I heard the affection in his voice and, for a moment, felt another surge of jealousy. "That's really sweet that you want to be close."

He raised an eyebrow. "Of course I want to be close to my daughter."

Had he said his daughter? So much for my astute skills of assumption. Was there even such a thing? "That was your daughter you were talking to?"

"Yeah, did you think . . . ?" He narrowed his eyes.

I raised a shoulder, ready to defend my position. "I just assumed it was a girlfriend."

"No, that was just my Chloe." He beamed as he said her name.

"And how old is she?" I asked, more curious than ever about my new coworker.

"Seven. She's the best thing to ever happen to me." He made another move in Jenga, and the tower wobbled before finding balance.

"You don't look old enough to have a seven-year-old."

He really didn't. I assumed he either had a girlfriend or liked to date around. He had an edgy, tough guy swagger. He wasn't scary tough, but he seemed like the type who could handle a gun, who liked to spit sunflower seeds, and who protected those in his circle—maybe all at once.

"I get that a lot. That's a story for another day."

The waitress set our food in front of us. The board was huge and artistically arranged. I started to salivate just looking at it.

Before I could grab a hot dog, a loud crash sounded outside.

As it did, the building shook, and our Jenga tower collapsed onto the table and floor.

Michael ran to the door and peered outside. I followed after him.

My mouth dropped open when I saw his minivan had been hit by another vehicle. The other driver sped away down the road.

What was going on?

CHAPTER NINE

Five minutes later, the cops had been called. Michael and I stood outside the restaurant along with a handful of other people and stared at his wrecked minivan. At least the weather was nice and sunny as we waited. The scent of the river floated around us, and the sound of boaters talking too loudly in the distance filled the air.

Why would someone ram a vehicle into Michael's? It made no sense.

"Did you see the vehicle that fled?" Michael asked me, turning away from the glaring sun.

I'd seen the vehicle, but it had been too far away for me to get a license plate or the make and model. "All I know is that it was a black sedan."

His gaze darkened as he shook his head. "That's all I could see too."

"Have you made anyone mad lately?" Wasn't that the only reason something like this would have happened? It seemed obvious to me that the act had been purposeful and out of vengeance. Michael had been targeted.

"I investigate people for a living, so I'm afraid my list is a little too long to narrow down right now." He rubbed his brow and looked away.

There was more to his story. I was certain of it.

"Could this be related to our investigation into Flash? Maybe we got a little closer to answers today than we thought."

Michael tilted his head, almost looking impressed. "Now you're thinking like an investigator. Maybe we did get a little too close and somebody wanted to send a message."

"If that camera we found offered a live feed . . . the person responsible for the crime could have been watching us. They could know we found it."

"And we could become targets," Michael finished.

Just then, an unmarked police car pulled into the lot. My eyes widened when I saw Detective Hunter step from the vehicle. I turned before he spotted me and I blew my cover.

"It's Hunter," I muttered. "I can't let him see me."

"Go inside. I can handle this."

Since I didn't witness the crime, hopefully the detective wouldn't need to talk to me.

Because that would be highly problematic.

I slipped inside the restaurant and stood near a window at the entrance, peering out.

I watched as Detective Hunter approached Michael with pen and paper in hand. From what I could tell, the detective appeared to be asking Michael for his version of the events. Then Hunter circled the vehicle several times and took some pictures.

Certainly, Michael knew that I couldn't be seen in this situation. Or did he? How much exactly did he know about this investigation and my secret undercover mission to find more answers?

I didn't know.

"Is everything okay, ma'am?" someone said behind me.

I turned and flashed my brightest smile to the blonde college-aged hostess standing behind the desk. "Just fine. Don't really like cops. I know it's weird."

That was my third lie. The first was when I told my mom about this job. The second was the lie of omission when I'd worked for the cleaning crew last night. How many lies was I going to have to tell in order to do this job?

"No, that's not weird at all. Plenty of people don't like cops. Was that your minivan that got smashed up?"

"Not mine but a colleague's."

"You mean Michael?"

"I guess you know him."

Her face darkened. "He doesn't need any more bad luck, does he?"

What did that mean? I supposed Michael would tell me if he wanted me to know. But I was more curious now than ever.

The hostess shook her head and sprayed the wooden stand in front of her with some Windex. "Man, is that a bummer."

"Tell me about it."

"I feel like I've seen that car before." She grabbed a paper towel and began wiping the area down. The woman wore a black T-shirt that proclaimed, "Old School Gamer." She had a nose ring, shaved hair at the sides of her head and longer on top, and some of the biggest plastic-framed glasses I'd ever seen.

My pulse quickened. "Say again?"

She nodded and continued sanitizing her station. "That's right."

I stepped closer to make sure I heard her correctly. "Did you see the driver?"

"Not really." She shrugged. "Sorry. There's a group that comes in to play Exploding Kittens about the same time every week. Their game is much more interesting."

"If you remember anything, can you call me? You'll probably need to tell the police that information also."

"Sure thing. Whatever I can do."

I wrote my name and number on the back of a business card—the restaurant's card, not mine. I wasn't that advanced yet.

As I glanced outside, I saw Detective Hunter get back into his car, and Michael started back this way.

I released my breath.

I'd just scraped by on this one. But living in a smaller

town was going to have its challenges. I needed to keep that in mind if I wanted to survive this new job.

Michael and I sat on the steps outside The Board Room waiting for the tow truck—that was forty-five minutes late—to come and for a rental car to pull up. The waitress had packaged up our charcuterie board and brought it out to us.

The hot dogs, even slightly cold, had been tasty.

I reminded myself not to adopt the American diet—not if I wanted to maintain my boyish figure. Food was so convenient here—and the more convenient it was, the less healthy. In Yerba, I'd gone to the market every day to get fresh fruits, vegetables, and bread.

It was already four o'clock, and I had to report to my new job by six. Not that I thought it would be a problem. But since I needed to take public transportation to get to these places . . . time was a consideration. I didn't want to blow this already.

"What a day, huh?" Michael pulled his hat off, ran a hand over his dark hair, and then returned the cap atop his head.

"You can say that again. I'm sorry about your minivan. You obviously get a lot of use out of it." That was my nice way of saying it was a pigsty.

"I'd like to say I hope the police catch this guy, but I don't have much hope of that."

"Maybe a traffic camera somewhere recorded his image. You never know."

"You're an optimist, aren't you?" Michael glanced at me, and I almost thought he felt sorry for me.

I'd have to examine that another time.

My gaze traveled across the gravel parking lot as a Bentley pulled up. A man stepped from the car and strode toward one of the boats in the distance.

My breath caught. It was the man who'd stopped and helped me yesterday. The one who had muttered what sounded like "mantente alerta." What was he doing here?

"Would you look at who that is?" Michael muttered, his gaze on Armani man. He didn't bother to hide the dislike in his voice.

"Should I know him?"

Michael glanced at me. "I forgot, you're new to this area. That, my friend, is Jono Harris. That's John-O, spelled J-o-n-o. Not the name he was born with, which was John Osborne. He thought Jono sounded more hip."

"Still not ringing any bells." Nada. None. Zilch.

"Oh, that's right, you also don't watch TV." He made a gun with his finger, pointed it at me, and fired. "Jono's father is undoubtably one of the wealthiest men on the East Coast. He works up in DC, but the family has a house here in Storm River. That's where Jono stays most of the time. Him and all his dates."

"Sounds like he has quite the reputation here in town." And like there was no love lost between the men.

Michael laughed. "Yeah, you could say that. There are lots of stories around town about Jono."

My curiosity peaked. "Like what?"

"I'll have to let you figure those out yourself. It will be more fun for you that way." A grin tugged at his lips. "One more mystery that you can solve."

"I'm sure the man can't be that interesting," I said.

Michael raised his eyebrows. "You might just be surprised."

Before we could talk anymore, the tow truck pulled up.

CHAPTER TEN

ichael dropped me back at my house so I wouldn't have to ride the bus again. That was a blessing. He'd also looked at my car for me and reconnected the spark plug wire again so I'd be able to drive to the apartment complex tonight.

He was turning out to be a lifesaver.

That was the one positive I could see in this somewhat sticky situation I'd gotten myself into.

As I walked into my house, I glanced at my watch and saw that I had only thirty minutes until I needed to meet the rest of the cleaning ladies. It didn't give me much time to get changed. Thankfully, my mom and my sister weren't home so I didn't have to explain everything to them.

I did have just enough time to do a little more research before I left, though.

On my computer, I quickly looked into Sarah Vance as

well as any of Flash's competitors who might want to put him out of commission.

On the Sarah Vance front, I hadn't found anything to indicate she'd been the target all along and Flash was just an innocent bystander. And, as far as Flash's competitors, none of them had stood out either.

At least I could mark those two research items off my list.

As soon as I got into my car and took off toward the apartment building, my phone rang. It was Oscar. Again. Yay for me.

I didn't want to answer, but I remembered all the rules that Velma had given me. The man may not take too kindly to me ignoring him.

I waited until I got to a stoplight and put the phone on speaker. Unfortunately, my car was too old for Bluetooth.

Putting on my most cheerful voice, I answered. "Hello, Oscar. How are you today?"

"Elliott," he barked. "I wanted to call and remind you of how important this task is today."

I resisted an eye roll. "Yes, I know."

"You need to find out something or Flash is going to be in prison for the rest of his life. No pressure, but there's a lot of pressure."

"I'm going to do my best."

"Your best may not be good enough. I thought I'd hired the right girl for this task. But you're going to need to prove that to me."

"I understand."

"Let me give you a little bit of advice, Dora," Oscar

continued. "Look like you're clueless. And, if you have to lie, make sure there's some truth in that lie. Got it?"

"I really hate lying." I frowned as I stared out my window.

"Then you're in the wrong line of work." He let out a deep chuckle. "I guess we're going to find out, huh?"

Part of me wanted to tell him I was going to quit. That I *was* the wrong person for this job.

Then I remembered his challenge. I didn't want anyone to tell me that I couldn't do something. I could get information tonight. I was capable.

A new determination rose inside me as I put my car into Park.

It was time to get down to business.

I lifted up a quick prayer. At the end of the day, I reminded myself, I had to live with myself. I couldn't do anything that went against my conscience. But in this job, that line seemed broken and quickly fading.

Two hours into the job, I finished cleaning the lobby. Then I'd moved into a resource room full of supplies like pens, pads of paper, and staplers.

Now I needed to hit the detective bureau area.

I wasn't mopping today. Apparently, that wasn't a daily thing. Today, I was simply running the vacuum and collecting trash.

I'd already run into Mr. Extroverted Cop Bradford. Our

supposed language barrier hadn't stopped him from blathering on and on to me again. He'd chatted about the weather and patrol duty and what he was doing when his shift ended.

I remembered that Oscar had told me I needed to get close to people. But I also wasn't supposed to speak English. It seemed like a contradiction. And even if language wasn't a barrier, I didn't want to use anyone so I could get ahead.

Finally, I finished working in this area and glanced at the spot where Detective Hunter's desk was located.

Three people worked here tonight, and most seemed preoccupied with their cases. I hadn't seen Detective Hunter yet. I didn't know much about the man, what cases he was really working, but something about the man caught my imagination.

I wondered about his life outside of work. About the woman whose picture I'd seen on his desk. If he was really an awful detective as Oscar Driscoll had said he was.

But right now, I really just needed to revel in the fact that Dylan Hunter wasn't here.

With a broom in one hand, I wandered closer to his desk. My gaze stopped on the photo there. The one of him with the pretty blonde. They looked so happy together.

I remembered feeling happy like that.

Emotion squeezed my heart.

I missed those days. I missed feeling the excitement of physical attraction. Of looking into Sergio's gaze and seeing the affection there. Of the anticipation of our future together.

It was the small things that got to me the most, though. Cooking together. Taking walks. Talking about our days.

But, right now, I needed to be focused.

I glanced around and confirmed that nobody was looking at me.

This was my opening.

Despite that, my heart pounded out of control. Was this the right thing?

If it allowed an innocent man to be cleared, then yes. I could see how my actions might be justified.

But if it compromised a police investigation, then that was an entirely different story.

My hands were sweaty as I reached forward. I made sure to stand with my back toward the door so my body blocked what I was doing.

There once was a girl that got caught. Her actions made her fraught. But she pushed on ahead, just like her boss said, and hoped she found what she sought.

With trembling hands, I pulled the file labeled VANCE from its holder on the desk.

Carefully, I flipped it open.

I was sweating so badly I feared a drop might fall from my forehead and onto the papers. DNA evidence.

However, they didn't check police files for DNA evidence. I knew this.

Right?

My anxiety caused me to not think clearly.

Dear Lord, I desperately want to ask You to help me. But I can't. It just doesn't feel right.

And that should be my first sign that I shouldn't be doing this.

I glanced down. I'd always had a good memory, and I hoped that my ability to retain facts didn't fail me now.

I scanned the text there, but most of it didn't make sense. Part of it was handwritten, and the scribble was so bad that it was hard to read anything.

I saw the words "Bernard Sutherland."

Who was he?

A few other phrases caught my eye. "Threatened caddy." "Short temper." "Loose cannon."

It sounded like the guy had given a statement on Flash's character.

"Can I help you?" a deep voice said behind me.

I gasped and turned around.

Dylan Hunter stood there staring at me.

I'd been caught.

CHAPTER ELEVEN

I pushed a hair behind my ear and flashed a nervous smile. "Hola, señor."

As I said the words, I turned, gently pushing the file back toward the holder where I'd found it.

"You're the same cleaner who was here yesterday." Detective Hunter narrowed his eyes as he studied me. "Can I help you?"

I stared at him, trying to pretend like I didn't understand a word he said. Then I said something in rapid-fire Spanish. "¿Quién hubiera adivinado que Capitán Americano vivía en Storm River?"

Yep. I'd said, "Whoever would have guessed that Captain America lived in Storm River?"

The sprint of words was becoming my go-to, as was avoiding eye contact and speaking nonsense.

The detective stared at me and shook his head, clearly not a Spanish speaker.

"You don't need to worry about my area." He pointed to his desk and shook his head. "No. . . . *bueno*. No . . . clean-o. Sweep-ese."

What did he think he was saying? Was this what was known as Spanglish?

As I stared at him, trying to look clueless, Rosa bustled in from the other room. She took my arm and led me away, muttering, *"Lo siento. Lo siento,"* to Hunter.

She was apologizing to him for whatever I'd done.

I glanced over my shoulder and saw the detective staring at us from his desk as we left the room.

Rosa must have seen the conversation from the other room. Her employment was on the line here, I realized.

I wouldn't ruin this for her.

If I ruined this for Oscar, he'd fail a client.

If I messed things up for Rosa, she could lose her livelihood.

More pressure pushed on me until I felt like I couldn't breathe.

Did the detective suspect I'd been looking at the file? I had no idea.

But suddenly I couldn't wait for this shift to end. I needed to get out of here and wrestle with my conscience until I could figure out what choice I could live with.

Almost as if Oscar was tracking my location, my phone rang as soon as I got back into my car after my shift was over. He wasn't tracking my location, right?

I shouldn't even have to ask myself that question. But his timing was uncanny—especially considering the fact that work had ended early tonight. It was only ten.

"Well?" he started.

I glanced in the rearview mirror, remembering that feeling I'd had earlier that someone was watching me. The skin on my neck crawled for a moment. Was the watcher back?

"Hola?" Oscar said. *"Guten tag?"*

I snapped my attention back to the phone call. "I'm here."

"Well? Did you learn anything?"

"I started to look into the folder, but the detective arrived before I could see much information."

Oscar muttered something under his breath before saying, "I told you that this is your *opportunidad.*"

I remembered what Michael said about Oscar's other assistants, and I knew I needed to be smart here. Should I tell him that I'd seen Bernard's name? I wasn't sure. I had no idea what the citation meant.

What was worse? Telling him I hadn't learned anything or telling him I'd learned something that might not mean much?

I decided to remain quiet, mostly because I didn't want to be scolded again. I simply needed to accept my failure. "I know you gave me a chance tonight, and I'm sorry I let you down."

"You need to go get your stuff from the office. Now."

The air left my lungs. "Tonight? It can't wait until morning?"

"No. You need to realize I'm a man of my word. I don't play."

My dad had also taught me to stand up for myself, and this man was being ridiculous right now. "Tonight wasn't my fault. I was trying to get the information when the detective came back. What was I supposed to do?"

"I'm not sure, but anything different than what you actually did. Need I remind you, Jungle Girl, that I'm paying you for all of this? Do you think I have money to waste?"

I flinched at his sharp words, but I still wasn't ready to back down. "I can only do what I can do."

"You know what that sounds like? An excuse. I don't want to see you in the morning. Am I clear?"

The call abruptly ended, and my head dropped back against my seat.

I couldn't believe this. Couldn't believe this job was over before it really even began—and now I had nothing.

I still had bills to pay. My mom and sister were depending on me. How was I going to tell them I was out of work?

I didn't know. But I was going to have to figure something out.

I didn't want to be the reason my sister couldn't get a new set of lungs.

I should have thought about that before I took this job.

I still felt the invisible weight pressing on my shoulders as I pulled up to the office building that I'd called mine for two whole days.

I didn't think I'd feel this disappointed about losing this job. Sure, I'd had a crisis of conscience over what I was doing. But, despite all of that, I liked to believe I was going to figure out a way to do things ethically somehow or another. I hadn't even had that chance. Just as I was starting to learn the ropes, I'd been cut loose.

Firing me hadn't been a fair move, but there was nothing I could do about it.

At the front door, I punched in an entry code I'd been given. But, as I opened the door, I heard something in the distance and froze.

I glanced behind me but saw nothing.

But I had definitely *heard* something.

The skin on my neck prickled.

I'd be a fool to ignore my instincts.

Moving more quickly, I stepped inside the office and twisted the lock behind me. As I stepped away from the door, my breaths came easier. Maybe I'd be safe. At least for a moment.

Right?

I glanced around, looking for any signs of trouble hiding in the shadows here. I saw nothing. Heard nothing. Sensed nothing.

But I still wanted to get done and get out of there. My nerves were frayed and ragged right now.

I hadn't brought many things into the office, but I did

have a picture of my family, a stress-relief ball, and a little plaque my best friend in Yerba had given me that read, "Embrace the Adventure." I wondered if Tahlia had any idea how those words were playing out right now.

As I started back toward the front door, I turned and looked at the office space one last time.

It seemed crazy that I was going to miss it so much. I didn't realize I'd become attached so quickly. But there were too many unanswered questions here, questions that had aroused my curiosity.

I hadn't gotten to know Velma very well yet, but part of me was sad that I wouldn't be able to get better acquainted with her. She seemed like the type that made life interesting. Why did she dumpster dive for food and work out at a sports equipment store?

And Michael . . . he seemed to have so many layers to him. I wanted to know more about his daughter, and his daughter's mom, and how he had gotten into this line of work.

Then there was Oscar. I wasn't really sure I wanted to get to know my former boss more. I wanted to believe that somewhere beneath all his insults was a good man who wanted to help people. Even though I had yet to see it, I hoped that trait was there.

What about Flash? Was he guilty of killing Sarah Vance or not?

Either way, the woman deserved justice. The internal pull to find answers was stronger than I'd ever anticipated.

But all of those things were now part of my past. Maybe it was for the best.

Truthfully, I should never have taken this job. I should have done something more expected of me like office work. Something boring but stable. Something that allowed me to live an expected life.

The strange thing was that part of me felt like there was a beast down inside me just waiting to emerge.

With one last glance at the dim space, I opened the door and stepped outside. No sooner had I done that did a shadow appear on my right.

Footsteps echoed on my left. I jerked my head toward the sound.

Oscar.

He walked this way.

I swerved my head back toward the shadow.

I sucked in a breath when I saw the gun protruding from the masked man's hand.

A gun that was aimed at Oscar.

Oh no . . .

I had to make a decision, and I had to make it quickly.

CHAPTER TWELVE

y new boss might be the biggest jerk to ever
walk the earth. Despite that, I knew what I
needed to do.

I lunged forward. My body collided with the masked man
in front of me, and we both fell to the ground. The man's gun
skittered across the sidewalk.

"Run!" I shouted to Oscar, glancing back at him. "Call the
cops!"

He froze for a moment. Then I heard his footsteps
hurrying away.

Realization washed over me.

Now it was just me and the gunman.

A dull throb played in my ears.

What had I been thinking?

Dear Lord . . . help me!

The man was still beneath me. He wore a black mask that

obscured his features. However, he smelled inebriated, and his eyes looked dazed.

At once, he shoved me back. My arm hit the sidewalk, and pain shot through me.

"You're going to regret that," the man growled as he popped to his feet.

The next instant, he reached across the stretch of cement and grabbed his gun.

My heart stuttered in my chest as time seemed to slow. Was he going to finish me off? And, if he did, what would that mean for my sister and mom? Who would help take care of Ruth?

My dad's face flashed through my mind. He'd be so disappointed with me. I knew how important it was to him that I help provide for the family, and I had failed. Maybe I should have thought this through instead of acting on instinct. Had there been another way I could have saved Oscar? It was too late to think about that now.

The gunman pointed his gun at me.

I squeezed my eyes shut, waiting in anticipation of the bullet that was sure to pierce my body. *God, I know I haven't been perfect. I know I need to do better. Please forgive me of my sins.*

I waited for the pain I felt certain would come.

But there was nothing.

I opened my eyes enough to see the man lower his arm and dart down the street.

I remained frozen a moment, unsure if I could believe my eyes.

Then I heard the sirens.

The man was gone.

Help was on the way.

Praise the Lord.

Footsteps approached from behind me. The next instant, Oscar knelt beside me.

"Are you okay?" he asked.

As I stared up at him, I had no idea what to say.

Because I might be alive . . . but I felt anything but okay.

Less than five minutes later, the police and paramedics had arrived. Even though I insisted I was fine, an EMT had checked me out and deemed that I was indeed okay. My arm and hip might be bruised from when I tackled the man, but I was otherwise in one piece.

I still wasn't sure what exactly I had been thinking when I took on that gunman by myself. Some type of internal instinct had just kicked in, I supposed. The reflex must have been lying dormant inside me because I'd had no idea it was even there.

Right now, I sat in the waiting area of Driscoll and Associates. Someone had brought me coffee. When I say someone, I meant Velma. She and Michael had also shown up. Oscar had probably called them.

Speaking of Oscar, the man was in his element right now, talking on the phone to a flock of reporters, as well as giving statements to the police. Too bad he hadn't been in his element when the man pulled out a gun.

Though my first instinct had been to protect him, where were Oscar's instincts? Did he not carry a gun?

The one piece of good news was that Detective Hunter had not shown up. Part of me had expected him to. But a man I'd never seen before had come instead. He'd introduced himself as Bellevue. I'd seen the man's name plate at the station. He sat two rows and one desk over from Hunter.

I wasn't sure how much longer I needed to stay here. The cops had already gotten my statement. Not only did I hate being the center of attention, but I really wanted to get home and check on my family.

"Are you sure you're doing okay?" Michael lowered himself in the leather chair beside me. He looked sleepy, like he'd just gotten out of bed and thrown on a blue sweatshirt. The heel of his loafers had collapsed, and he wore them almost like slippers.

I nodded.

"It was awfully brave what you did back there."

"Or stupid. It was most likely stupid."

He didn't argue with me. "There's no telling who that man was. Oscar has a long list of enemies, even longer than my own list. It's something that happens when you work this job for too long."

"I bet."

"Either way, you probably saved Oscar's life."

"I guess that can be my one good deed before I say goodbye to this place."

Michael stared at me and squinted. "What do you mean say goodbye? Did you quit?"

"Oscar fired me." I glanced across the building and through the open door into Oscar's office. The man was still preoccupied, talking on the phone with someone and making larger-than-life hand motions. "I figured you knew."

"Why in the world would he fire you?" Michael's voice rose with emotion.

"I didn't find out as much information at the police station as he anticipated I would, and therefore I am deemed a failure at life." Okay, I may have overstated that.

Michael rolled his eyes. "Oscar can be out of control at times. He had no right to fire you. You did great work today. We wouldn't have found that camera if you hadn't been there."

"I appreciate your encouragement, but apparently Oscar doesn't see it that way."

Michael glanced at Oscar, and his eyes narrowed. "I'm going to talk to him."

As he popped to his feet and started that way, I grabbed his arm. "You don't have to do that. You have a family to take care of. Don't put yourself on the line for me."

Michael shook his head, his jaw hardening. "I can't let him be a bully. There are certain lines that can't be crossed."

"But—"

"This isn't your decision." Michael's intense gaze latched onto mine. "It's mine."

As Michael stormed over to Oscar, Velma left her desk and took his place beside me. Worry lined her forehead, and she held out a case of mints. "Would you care for one?"

"Where did they come from, if you don't mind me asking?"

"Oscar gave them to me."

I assumed they were safe and took one from the container, popping it into my mouth. The cooling mint somehow made me feel calmer.

"I refilled the tin with some mints this lady at a restaurant threw away," Velma said. "Don't worry—they weren't buried deep in the trashcan."

I froze, wanting to spit the mint out. But it was already in my mouth. Any germs had already done their damage.

With a stiff jaw, I shoved the mint to the side of my mouth to let it dissolve. But I really shouldn't ever take any food from this woman. Ever.

"I can't believe all of this happened," Velma shook her head, her dangly earrings chiming.

Despite the late-night call, somehow she had time to put her earrings in. Or was she the type who hadn't settled in for the night yet? I wasn't sure.

"You mean, it's not a normal day in the life of a PI?" I held my breath as I waited for her response.

"No, not at all. I mean, Oscar did get some death threats after the Ernesto case. But that was several years ago, and I thought all of that had passed."

"I had no idea this line of work was so . . . exciting, for lack of a better word."

"It usually isn't. But, every once in a while, Oscar gets a good case, the kind that stirs things up."

Noticing movement, I glanced around. Were the police

and reporters leaving? Were things wrapping up? That's how it appeared.

The detective stepped from Oscar's office, nodded at me, and then stepped out the door, followed by two patrol officers.

I stood, relieved that this might be over. "You know, I really don't think I'm needed here anymore. And I am exhausted. I've been on my feet all day, and I haven't been home. I think I'm going to take off. Can you tell everybody I said goodbye?"

"You're not going anywhere, Dora," a deep voice bellowed.

I froze as I saw Oscar approach me. I said nothing, only waited. Was that a threat? His tone certainly hadn't sounded kind.

Speaking of which, I'd looked up Dora earlier, while I'd been waiting for the police to arrive. I'd realized she was a cartoon jungle explorer. Oscar had meant the words as a veiled insult, hadn't he?

"I made a mistake." He stopped in front of me. "It takes a lot for me to say that, but I did. You saved my life tonight, and I need to say *gracias*."

The man was actually apologizing? Now I just needed to see a flying anaconda. Both held the same likelihood.

"You're welcome. I'd like to think you'd do the same for me." Even though I said the words, I wasn't sure there was any truth in them.

"I shouldn't have fired you. What can I do to convince you to stay?" Oscar stared at me, his intimidating stance not matching his words.

My mind raced. Part of me wanted to say that being fired was the best thing that could've happened to me. It had given me an out. No longer would I have to wrestle with moral choices as to whether or not I could do the job. No longer would I have to lie to my mom.

Something else wouldn't let the words leave my mouth. I hadn't felt this alive in so long. I didn't want to go back to a desk job. I didn't want the ordinary, the predictable, the boring. Working this case had lit a fire in me that I didn't know was there.

Instead, I was just as surprised as anybody when I said, "I'll stay, but I need a raise."

As Oscar stared at me, everybody in the office went silent.

I had no idea how my boss would respond to my demand or if I'd just permanently messed up my chances of working here longer.

Finally, his face twitched. "Fine."

"And don't call me Dora."

"Okay."

"And don't treat me like I'm beneath you because I'm a foreigner and a woman."

"But—"

"I mean it. No buts."

"Fine." Oscar scowled. "I know quality when I see it. Good employees are hard to find. We'll talk more in the morning. Actually, for that matter, why don't you wait until around lunchtime to come in? You've had a long day."

"Thank you." I released my breath. I couldn't believe my negotiations had actually worked.

I stood, ready to leave. Before I even reached the door, Michael joined me.

"I'll walk you out." He fell in step beside me as we walked on the sidewalk to my car.

"You didn't have to do that with Oscar," I told him. "Pleading my case could have gotten you fired."

"I only did it because I meant what I told him. You have a lot of potential. It would be a big mistake to let you go now."

It felt good to hear that someone believed in me. "Thank you."

We paused by my car. Michael stared at me, something swirling in his gaze. Was that sincerity? Admiration? Curiosity? Maybe it was a mix of all three.

"I mean it. You did good work today. You're a little different. But it's in a good way. I think you could really bring some good change around here, Elliot."

"Thanks, Michael." I offered a smile. "Good night."

Ever since I'd moved here, I'd prayed that God would send me a friend. I'd assumed it would be a female. But what if Michael was my answer to prayer? Out of everyone I'd met, he seemed the closest to understanding me, and he was so easy to talk to.

Only time would tell me the answer to that question.

But my heart felt lighter as I climbed into my car.

CHAPTER THIRTEEN

'd gotten back home and muttered good night to my mom. I'd called her earlier to let her know I'd be late because something had come up. Miraculously, she hadn't asked that many questions.

I'd escaped to the shower to get the scent of Clorox and Electric Youth off me. As I stood under the spray, I remembered seeing the gun. I remembered the realization that I was alone with a dangerous man twice my size with no backup plan.

Fear hit me again, and my lungs tightened.

I wished I could wash away the memories.

Instead, I turned the water off and dried my skin.

Then I sat in bed, surprisingly not tired. I had too much on my mind.

I picked up the jewelry box again. It seemed to be my go-to when I felt stressed. Somehow feeling the wood beneath my fingers reminded me of my dad.

What would he tell me right now? Would he say to run far away from Oscar Driscoll? To get a respectable job? I wasn't sure.

He'd always had a gleam of adventure in his eyes. He'd been a jungle guide when my mother met him. He'd go on month-long trips with tourists who wanted to explore the Amazon.

When he'd gotten married, he'd decided to take a government job. Though there was still some travel, it wasn't nearly as much. Once, he'd told me it was quiet, boring work, mostly behind a desk.

Papa had told me I was a good person for working behind the scenes. For supporting those in power. For helping organizations run smoothly.

Now that I'd had a taste of what it was like not to play it safe, I didn't want to return to living in the background. I wanted to feel alive again.

I opened one of the drawers again. Part of me wished I had something inside. But this drawer was empty. The one above it had some costume jewelry from Yerba, but I only wore it on special occasions.

I opened a door on the side of the jewelry box and touched one of the necklace hooks. I tugged on it and imagined hanging something there. Maybe a simple gold chain with a diamond pendant at the end. Not a huge rock. Maybe a half a carat, at most.

As my finger lingered there, something popped.

Had I broken it? The way my day was going, it wouldn't surprise me.

As I looked at the bottom of the case, I noticed a piece of edging had come off.

I squeezed my eyes shut. Yes, the one material object in this life that was important to me I'd somehow managed to mess up.

As I tried to press it back in place, I realized that it wasn't a piece of trim at all. It was actually a hidden drawer disguised as edging.

I could hardly breathe as I pulled it out.

That's when I saw a little leather-bound journal inside.

My heart pounded in my ears.

I gently lifted the book out and muttered a quick prayer before opening the worn cover. As soon as I saw the words on the front page, I knew that whatever was inside was going to change my world.

"My precious *bambina*," my father started.

I held back tears as I read the words in my father's familiar scrawl. *Precious bambina.* That's what he'd always called me, using a mix of Spanish and English.

I closed my eyes as realization rolled over me.

My father had left this here for me. Hidden. On purpose.

He'd wanted me to eventually find it.

Questions swirled in my head, and I kept reading.

If you have found this, there's a good chance that I am no longer alive. I want you to know how much I love you, your mama, and your sister. You all are the whole world to me.

But I have not always been truthful with you.

I paused. My dad not truthful? That didn't fit everything he'd ever taught me. He was the one who'd drilled into me why honesty and integrity were so important.

The truth is, I didn't work as a diplomat for the intelligence wing of our government. For the past ten years, I've worked as a spy, and I've made a lot of enemies. It was just one more reason why I had to get you and the rest of the family out of the country. There are people who want me dead.

I sucked in a shallow breath. What? Had I read that correctly?

I know I put too much on you. I know you probably feel pressured to help pay bills, to help with Ruth. I'm so sorry for that. But I also know that you always do the right thing.

I'm counting on you to do that now.

The way he wrote the words . . . it almost sounded like he knew he might die. That couldn't be possible, right? But what sense did all of this make?

My head spun for a moment until his words came back into focus.

I need you to protect your mother and sister. I've always seen those qualities in you, but I tried to suppress them. That's why I encouraged you to get a job as chief of staff, something behind the scenes. Otherwise, I was afraid that you might follow in my foot-steps. While I knew you'd excel in the field, I also knew that it would put you in danger. I couldn't stand the thought of that.

But the time for those things is gone now. I'm afraid my enemies are now targeting my family. So I've written down everything that you need to know about protecting your mom and sister and . . . staying alive.

I swallowed hard. This hadn't been what I expected.

My family? In danger?

Fear squeezed me. What in the world was I going to do?

CHAPTER FOURTEEN

"So you *are* alive."

I looked up from the table where I ate some toast before I headed into work. My sister stood there, dressed for school and staring at me. "I know I've been busy this week. I'm sorry."

"You must really like this new job." She lowered herself across from me at the wobbly kitchen table.

Ruth was a beautiful girl. She always had been, from the time she was just a baby. She had beautiful light-brown hair, with natural blonde highlights, that she kept long and wavy. She had a slim figure and a great smile. To look at her, most people wouldn't realize she had a life-altering disease.

I reminded myself that she and my mother thought I was working for an attorney. "I do like the job."

Guilt gnawed at me again. I really should tell them the

truth, but I couldn't stand to see my mom worry any more than she already did.

Speaking of my mom, she was in her bedroom teaching online English lessons to students overseas. The extra job helped to bring in enough money every week to buy some groceries and to pay the electric bill, at least.

"You seem different." Ruth examined the tips of her hair for split ends. "Is something going on? Did you meet somebody?"

"Meet somebody?" I let out an airy laugh. "No, I definitely did not meet anybody."

Unless a potential killer counted.

"All these people here in Storm River, and you haven't met a soul yet, huh? Let me guess—no one can take Sergio's place." She scowled. She'd never liked him.

"Most of the people here in Storm River are not my type of people."

She made duck lips as she let her head fall to the side. "Why? Because they're rich?"

"That's definitely part of it."

"You're not judging, are you?" She widened her eyes and changed her voice to mock horror.

I started to retort that it was impossible to judge a rich person. Then I realized the dishonesty in my words and stopped myself. It didn't matter if you were judging people with less than you or more than you. A judgment was still a judgment.

"You're right. I'm sure there are nice people here. I'm just not sure that there are people here who share my values." I took another bite of my toast and swallowed it. "Speaking of which, how are things going at school?"

"The people here are not my type of people," my sister said, keeping her expression placid.

I balled my napkin and threw it at her. A smile cracked her face, and she let out a laugh.

"In all seriousness, I like it," she said. "But I miss hanging out with you. I wish this new job didn't make you work so much."

"It's not always going to be like this. But I'm just getting my feet wet and learning the ropes. That means that I gotta put in some extra time. The good news is that I get paid by the hour so we should be able to pay all our bills this month."

My sister reached across the table and squeezed my hand, her fussy teenager persona disappearing for a moment. "I know the only reason you work so hard is because you want to take care of me. I wish that you were able to chase your own dreams."

"My dreams mean nothing if you're not there with me as a part of them." My voice caught.

I meant the words. My sister, even though she was younger than I by ten years, was one of my best friends. I couldn't imagine life without her. That meant I needed to keep her healthy and safe.

As I remembered the words I'd read in my dad's journal last night, his message was driven home even more.

He had enemies who would like to see us dead.

My heart stuttered.

Did that explain why I felt like I was being watched sometimes? It seemed like a logical explanation to me. But, even if I did need help, whom was I supposed to turn to? Whom could I trust to keep that secret and watch my back? I had no idea. In fact, right now I felt all alone as I faced this.

I was still trying to comprehend everything that my dad had said in the journal entry I'd read. I'd read only the first two pages, but I'd skimmed the rest. He'd laid out a guidebook for what I needed to do, measures I needed to take.

I'd decided to only read one entry a day. That was all I could comprehend.

Even though I'd been ready to quit my new job with Oscar, I now realized that I needed to learn how to be more street smart. Working for the PI just might be the perfect job for me to do that.

My sister snatched my last piece of toast and stood, hoisting her book bag over her shoulder. "I'm going to be late for school. You behave yourself today."

"Yeah, you do the same." I smiled as I watched her walk away. Before Ruth reached the door, a coughing fit seized her.

My smile disappeared.

How much longer did she have until she needed that new lung transplant? The doctors couldn't give us an exact time. They just said it would need to be soon.

I had fifteen hundred dollars saved up right now. But I wasn't sure that would be enough to get us through.

Then I remembered Jono with his expensive clothes and

car. Someone like him could spend that much money in a day and not even blink an eye.

Life just didn't seem fair sometimes.

Life *wasn't* fair. But sitting here and feeling sorry for myself was going to do nothing.

I stood from the table. It was only seven o'clock, but I was going to go into work.

I couldn't wait to find out where we were on the Flash Slivinski case.

Thinking about his problems definitely beat thinking about my own.

***

"I've been doing some research on Art Smith," Michael started as he sat at his desk, clicking away on a laptop computer.

Everyone was already here by the time I arrived—and I hadn't even come in late like Oscar had told me.

Oscar brought us coffee—even me. I must be predictable. He'd known I'd be here on time, hadn't he? Velma brought in donuts I couldn't eat—Michael warned me not to. And as I stared at a stray piece of wilted lettuce on the box, I knew his advice was sound.

She'd probably gotten these out of a dumpster.

In other words, everything seemed normal—except Oscar was being a little nicer than usual.

I glanced across the office at Oscar's door. "Shouldn't we

bring Oscar in on this meeting? Won't he want to hear any updates?"

Michael looked at me as if I'd just asked an absurd question. "No, why would we do that?"

"Because, isn't he the private eye on the case? I mean, I'm not even licensed. We might do the footwork, but he calls the shots. Right?"

"I am actually licensed. And you might have thought I was exaggerating when I said Oscar was just a figurehead. But I wasn't. At one time, he was a great PI. He lost himself in alcohol and fame."

My respect for the man continued to decrease, which I didn't think was possible.

I sighed and leaned back, staring at the chocolate-covered donut in front of me. I really wanted to eat it still, but I had to choose my battles. Instead, I needed to focus on this case.

"Okay," I started. "Who is Art Smith?"

"I thought you'd never ask." Michael turned his screen toward me. "Art Smith works out of New York City. He's thirty-six, and he's an attorney."

"That doesn't tell me one single thing about why he fits in with any of this."

"I'm getting to that." Michael picked up an orange from his desk and began tossing it in the air. He apparently juggled when he had energy to burn. "It turns out he has a connection with our friend Flash Slivinski."

I leaned forward, suddenly intrigued. "Is that right?"

"True fact. You see, Art Smith is not only an attorney, but he's an attorney for Windsor Washington Golf Clubs."

"Okay . . ." I waited for Michael to continue his thought. I realized it must somehow tie in with Flash's career, but I didn't know how.

"Flash has an endorsement deal with Windsor Washington Golf Clubs. But lately, he's been giving the company some bad press. He was caught on video saying that their products were inferior. Of course, he later apologized and explained that his words had been taken out of context. But the damage had already been done."

"So why didn't the company just drop him?"

"Because, apparently, they were going to have to pay out more money in order to do that. Law and contracts are complicated, especially when it comes to endorsement deals. They would lose money either way."

I processed that before saying, "So you think this company is looking for another excuse as to why Flash needs to be dropped from the contract, one that will change the legal ramifications?"

Michael caught the orange and held it in his hands. "Bingo!"

I didn't feel as confident as he did. "But do you think that this Art guy would go as far as to kill Flash's date so he could save his company some money? It sounds extreme."

"I don't want to believe that, but I've seen far crazier things happen. I feel like it should be checked out at least."

I leaned back, trying to think things through and be open-minded. "Okay, but what about that camera that we found at Flash's place? Did you make any headway?"

"I've been working on that." Michael turned back to his

computer. "It's all digital so whatever was being recorded was sent to some kind of server. I'm trying to figure out exactly whose server that might be. The owner of the site has some great firewalls that are nearly impossible to get through."

"So we're not going to get anywhere with that, huh?"

Michael raised his shoulder. "I didn't say that. I am pretty good at this, if I do say so myself. But I don't have any answers—yet."

"Last question—what about the man who hit your car? Do the police have any leads?"

"I called this morning, and the answer was . . . no. Not surprising. I don't expect they'll find anyone. For someone to pull something like that in broad daylight . . . they knew what they were doing, especially since cops patrol the area quite often. This guy just happened to hit between police drive-bys."

"That's too bad."

Michael looked at me. "How about you? Any updates?"

I straightened. "I did see one thing when I was at the police station last night, but I'm not sure if it's significant. I didn't even tell Oscar because I didn't want to set him off."

His eyes lit with curiosity. "What's that?"

"The name Bernard Sutherland. Does that ring any bells?"

Excitement raced through Michael's eyes. "As a matter of fact, it does. Bernard Sutherland is Flash's manager."

I sucked in a breath at the revelation. "His name was listed in Sarah Vance's file. You think that police are investigating him as a possible suspect?"

"Did it say anything else?"

"Something about loose cannon and the word 'caddy' had been scribbled. I'm not sure what all that means, though."

"I'd say it's something worth looking into. But, first, let's start with Art and work our way down."

CHAPTER FIFTEEN

Twenty minutes later, Michael and I were in Oscar's BMW, headed toward one of the many country clubs in Storm River. Michael's minivan was in the shop, and my car wouldn't have been believable at the expensive venue, so we'd borrowed our boss's.

I'd touched up my makeup and pulled my hair back into a neat bun before we left. Michael had pulled on a Polo shirt and khakis. However, he hadn't lost his hat or skater shoes. He could get away with the look. It somehow fit his laid-back vibe.

Founders Circle Golf and Country Club was only about five minutes away from Oscar's office. It was amazing how such a short distance could change things. Don't get me wrong—the area where Oscar's office was located was nice and refined, as was the rest of Storm River.

But as soon as you crossed to this side of Main Street, the

town became the playground of millionaires. Most of the homes had to be more than six thousand square feet. There were four golf clubs, and yachts lined the inlet coming from the river. I'd never felt so out of place.

A gated fence stretched around the grounds of the club, allowing only members and their guests to enter. That would be challenge number one. But it wasn't surprising. This was typical Storm River, designed with the hoity-toity in mind.

"Just remember to play it cool and follow my lead," Michael said.

Despite his words, sweat formed across my skin. How was I ever going to pull this off? I wasn't a country club girl. In some ways Oscar was right. I'd rather be tracking through the jungle and exploring nature than coming to a place like this.

"You're getting nervous." Michael gave me a side glance.

"Is it that easy to see that I'm ready to—" I paused and cleared my throat before adding, "flee."

He shrugged. "Maybe a little. You have to get those impulses under control. You can be nervous, just don't show it."

"I'm trying. I really am." I rubbed my hands against my jeans.

As we pulled up to a station near the gate, Michael rolled down his window and flashed what almost appeared to be a cultured smile. "My wife and I are interested in placing our membership here at the club, and we were hoping to get a tour."

The guard, a man who wore a fitted suit and a matching

uptight expression, stared at us with obvious distaste in his eyes. "We only accept new guests by appointment. I'm sorry to have wasted your time."

"Unfortunately, this is the only time we're available for a tour. Is there any way that the rules might be bent?" Michael sounded amiable and kind, tapping into the side of him that made him sound like everyone's best friend.

"I'm sorry. We don't bend the rules for anybody." The guard still sounded uptight and snooty.

"What if I slipped you a little something?" A fifty-dollar bill magically appeared in Michael's hand.

The man let out a haughty laugh. "I'm sorry, but we cannot be bought here. We like to maintain the utmost integrity in all of our dealings. Now if you would run along."

He nodded at the car behind us, indicating that there were more important people waiting to get in.

Michael exchanged a look with me and narrowed his eyes.

We both knew this wasn't going to work. After a moment of hesitation, Michael turned the car around, and we headed away.

Only we didn't.

Michael pulled onto a street nearby and parked the BMW.

"What are you doing?" I sensed he had another plan up his sleeve.

"I'm going to teach you a little bit about surveillance."

"I'm not sure how surveillance is going to help us in this situation. We need to talk to this guy."

"I know. But we need to *surveil* him until we can find the opportunity to *speak* with him."

I nodded toward the rolling green hills of the golf course. "That place is huge. I'm not sure how you think you're going to be able to locate Art inside and surveil him."

"We'll figure out a way." Michael reached into the backseat and grabbed a duffle bag. "Come on."

Before I had a chance to ask any more questions, he was out the door and headed down the sidewalk. I scrambled to keep up with him, wondering just what was in store.

Part of me couldn't wait to find out.

Michael stopped near a row of cherry blossom trees that lined the white fencing around the golf course. He sat on a bench on the sidewalk with the bag beside him and slipped on some sunglasses.

I still wasn't sure how this was going to prove anything.

"So how do we find Art in there?" I always liked having a plan. It was just my personality. Winging it—and/or being in the dark—wasn't my thing.

"I'm checking his social media right now." Michael pulled out his phone. "I'm not really sure how investigators did things before the era of Facebook and Twitter."

I sat beside him and glanced over his shoulder. "I wouldn't know. I'm not on social media."

He stopped and stared at me. "Really?"

I nodded. "I think it's a waste of time. I prefer face-to-face interactions. I find them more meaningful. And, if those things don't work, reading a book is always a good choice."

"You're an interesting girl, Elliot Ransom."

"Thank you?" That was the second time he'd said something like that, and I still wasn't sure how to interpret it.

As Michael continued to scroll through postings, I glanced at his bag and wondered what was inside. Telephoto lenses, perhaps? Beef jerky and water? I had no idea.

"There he is." Michael held up his phone and showed me a picture. "Just two minutes ago Art posted a photo on Twitter, tagging himself in front of the west wing of the Founders Circle Country and Golf Club. He was sporting his handy-dandy Windsor Washington golf clubs, of course."

"Do you know where that area of the golf course is?"

Michael stood. "As a matter of fact, I do. Follow me."

Just as before, he took off at a quick clip, and I could hardly keep up.

I wondered how he knew so much about this place. He didn't seem like the golfing type or a country club regular. But I'd save those questions for another day.

He rounded the corner and an identical sidewalk came into view. Michael found another bench by another tree and put his bag down again. Except this time, he reached inside and pulled something out.

I stared for a moment. Were those binoculars? Weren't passersby going to raise questions if they saw him using those in broad daylight?

"I need you to help me not be seen," he started.

"And how am I supposed to do that?" Did I really want to know?

"I need you to distract anybody who might walk past."

"How exactly do you expect me to distract them?" I could do a dance from the Festival of the Chicken, but I wasn't sure that's what he had in mind.

He shrugged. "You'll figure it out."

A swell of nerves rose in me. "You do realize I'm an introvert, right? This isn't in my skillset."

"This is the age of the introvert. You'll be fine."

"Age of the introvert?"

"Yes, the rise of the introvert has been well documented. It's cool to be introverted. Just don't use that as a crutch. Now, I'd talk you through it more, but we don't have any time to waste."

He glanced up and down the street, before putting the binoculars to his eyes and peering at the golf course in the distance.

All of this fascinated me. I wondered if my dad had done things like this before. Did I really have the *habilidades* to follow in his footsteps? Did being the sidekick to a private investigator count as following in the footsteps of an international agent of intrigue?

I had so many questions.

I ran my sweaty hands over my jeans as I glanced around.

It was a beautiful day, just the kind of day that might send people out to wander the sidewalks. The good news was this side of town didn't contain any of the quaint shops that other parts of town did. Across the street, residential homes stood tall and broad.

With any luck, I would walk away from this without having to embarrass myself.

But as soon as that thought entered my head, a man and a woman strolled around the corner arm in arm. They were probably in their fifties and reminded me of a couple who'd just come from a horse race. She wore an oversized hat, and the man had a handlebar mustache that made him look like he'd stepped out of another century.

My gut twisted with anxiety. This was it. This was when I needed to distract them before they called the police on us for being Peeping Toms. Me and my introverted self could do this.

I tried to get over myself as I stepped toward them. I knew a simple conversation wouldn't do. If I was too calm and demure, all they would do was glance around and pay only half attention to me. I needed something big.

But not a chicken dance. *Resist the chicken dance.*

"Did you see that?" I pointed behind them.

The couple turned. The woman clutched her purse as if she was afraid this was some kind of scam.

In some ways, it was, but I wasn't going to tell her that.

"See what?" A hint of annoyance laced the man's voice.

"It was a very rare fulvous whistling duck." I wanted to clamp my mouth shut as soon as the words left my lips.

A fulvous whistling duck? They didn't even have those in North America.

"I don't see anything." The woman craned her neck, trying to catch a glance.

"It just flew behind those houses over there. They're super rare. In fact, if you're lucky enough to see one, it's supposed to bring you good luck and great fortune." I made that part up.

That seemed to get the woman's attention. She raised her eyebrows and glanced at the man with her. "We could always use more of that."

"Couldn't we all?" I said with a little laugh.

I wondered if Michael was done yet. I couldn't afford to glance back at him and check, though. I didn't want to draw any attention to him.

"I am sorry that I interrupted your walk," I continued. "I just believe in sharing in abundance."

The man and woman glanced at each other again, as if that concept was foreign.

They were obviously tired of this conversation because they skirted around me and started to continue on their way.

Should I try to keep them here longer? What else could I possibly say?

Thankfully, before I put myself through anymore of this humiliation, I felt an arm around my shoulder.

"I saw it, honey." Michael held up the binoculars and pulled me close. "It's a great day for birdwatching."

The man and the woman offered another tight smile before hurrying on their way.

As soon as they were out of earshot, I released my breath.

"Good job." Michael stepped away from me, our charade over. "You picked a topic that played right in with binoculars. Quick thinking."

I didn't bother to mention to him that it had been an accident.

"But a very rare fulvous whistling duck?" He raised his eyebrows.

I shrugged. "I knew it had to be something unique and . . . I just didn't know what else to say."

"You did fine."

Maybe, but I still felt a little rattled. "How about you? Did you see anything?"

He slipped the binoculars from around his neck and stuck them back in his leather bag. "As a matter of fact, I did. I was able to spot Art. He's playing a round of golf right now. By the time he reaches the eighth hole, he's going to be close enough for us to talk to him."

"That sounds perfect. But we're not going to be playing golf."

"That's why we're going to need another distraction." He handed his skater hat to me. "You're going to need to wear this. I don't have lice. I promise."

I had no idea what he had up his sleeve, but I slipped the hat on.

CHAPTER SIXTEEN

s we waited for Art to make it to the eighth hole, Michael and I sat on the bench with nothing but time to kill.

"So how do you know so much about this country club?" I asked.

He shrugged again, and I saw the hesitation in his eyes. The man was a mystery on so many levels. Was he the innocent, playful boy next door? The dedicated father? Or did he have a wild past, complete with a come-to-Jesus moment?

I still wasn't sure.

"Let's just say I worked here for a little while." Michael pushed his sunglasses up higher on his nose. "True fact."

"You're a local?" Another surprise. There was so much I didn't know about this guy.

"I never intended to be. In fact, I moved up to New York City as soon as I was old enough to get out of town. But that all changed, and now I'm back here. I realized I couldn't do this single parenting thing without some support. My mom and dad were more than gracious and allowed me to come back home."

"I see. That's great that you have them close. I'm sure it helps a lot."

"It really does."

"Does Chloe's mom have a lot to do with her?" The question was probably too personal, but I asked anyway.

"I haven't seen Roxy since Chloe was two months old."

My eyes widened. "Wow. I had no idea."

"It's just one of those things . . . sometimes you wish you could go back in time and give yourself a good talking to. Then again, I wouldn't trade Chloe for anything in the world. Great things can come from the mistakes we make."

Wise words. "If you don't mind me asking, what were you doing up in New York City?"

"I'd tell you, but you might laugh." He rubbed the Jesus tattoo on his fingers.

"You might be surprised. Oscar thinks I'm a living, breathing Dora the Explorer, apparently. There are so many parts of my past that no one here relates to or understands."

Michael stared off in the distance, and I was certain he wasn't going to tell me anything else. Then he cleared his throat and straightened just slightly. "I played major league baseball for a few years."

"Wow. That's . . . great." I'd never met anyone who'd told me that. "What happened?"

"I got too heavy into the partying. Drinking. I lost my

contract. When Chloe was born, I realized I had to get myself straight."

My heart lodged in my throat. I wouldn't have guessed any of those things about Michael. But we all had our pasts, didn't we? There were things we were proud of and things we wished we could hide away forever. That was just a part of growing up and maturing.

"So I told you all about me." Michael turned toward me. "Now why don't you tell me something interesting about you? I know that your mom was a missionary and that she met your dad down in some country that I've hardly ever heard of, but I do believe is real."

"It's very real. Believe me." I drew in a deep breath as I contemplated what to say.

"Tell me something new." He casually stretched his arm across the back of the bench, the action making his broad chest seem even broader.

He did have the build of a baseball player, I realized.

My mind went back to the journal my dad had left. I wasn't ready to talk about that yet. Not with anybody. Not with my mom, my sister, and definitely not with this man that I'd only met yesterday. But it would be so nice to talk to *someone*.

"I graduated at the top of my class and was voted most likely to succeed. Granted, there were only seventy-five people in my graduating class, but still . . ."

"College?"

"I studied international affairs. I had a job lined up before I even graduated."

"You're an achiever."

"I am. I actually just took the enneagram personality test. My sister made me, and that's the exact label she gave me. Now she keeps calling me a three. What are you?"

"An enthusiast. Or, an eight, as your sister might say."

"That doesn't surprise me."

"I figured it wouldn't." He shifted, his smile disappearing. "What was it like being there when the political corruption started?"

I swallowed hard again as I remembered those days. "It was scary. There were riots. Innocent men died. People we knew. Families turned on each other. I never thought I'd see anything like that. The unrest started a decade ago. But every time it flared up, it would eventually die. Until recently. Everything seemed to explode."

"I can't even imagine. Did you say that's why you left?"

"Partly. But the primary reason was because my sister has cystic fibrosis and the treatments here are so much better than in Yerba."

He nodded slowly. "That makes sense."

I glanced down at my hands. "My dad passed away right after we moved here. A heart attack. Now it's just my mom, sister, and me. It's not exactly the ideal situation, but we're all doing what we can to make ends meet."

"I think that's really great that you're helping your mom and sister out. We all need people to give us a hand sometimes."

I nodded slowly. "Yeah, I guess we do."

Before we could talk anymore, Michael's phone screen lit.

He'd set an alert to let us know when Art posted online again.

"It says Art just showed up at the eighth hole."

I touched the hat on my head. "So what is this for? Can you tell me yet?"

"You'll see." A twinkle formed in his eyes. "Come on."

I wondered what exactly was in store, and I prayed I didn't blow it.

I watched as Art and two other men took their place at the eighth hole. The fence was close enough to them to work in our favor. That was the good news.

The bad news was that I was still a little anxious about what Michael had in store for us.

"Here goes nothing," he leaned closer and whispered.

The next thing I knew, he flipped the hat from atop my head, and it went flying with the breeze over the fence.

"Oh, man!" Michael made a big production out of peering over the pickets and onto the greens below. "I'm sorry to interrupt your game, but my girlfriend's hat just blew over there. Would you mind getting it for me?"

I watched carefully, curious about who would retrieve it. It was really a matter of chance, wasn't it? Michael's plan might not work.

But out of all three of the men, Art was the youngest. The other two appeared to be in their sixties or seventies.

Michael's bet paid off.

Art walked toward the wayward hat and grabbed it for us. He flipped his hand out to give it back to Michael, a shiny, white smile on his face. "Here you go."

"Thanks, man. I appreciate it."

Art had only taken two steps away when Michael called him again.

"Hey, didn't I see you before? At the Green Leaf Tavern maybe?"

Art froze.

I watched, soaking everything in, desperate to learn the tricks of the trade.

"Sorry. I don't think I've ever been there before." Art started to turn away again.

"No, I'm nearly positive it was you," Michael said. "I remember your hair. It reminds me of John F. Kennedy Jr.'s. Impressive, by the way."

Irritation crossed Art's features. "I'm sorry, but I think you've mistaken me for someone else."

"As a matter of fact, I think you were there the day Flash Slivinski was, right before the murder."

That got Art's attention. He glanced at his golf buddies before walking closer to us and lowering his voice. "What kind of game are you playing here? What do you want from me?"

"We just have a few questions," Michael said, remaining coolly unflustered.

"Who sent you?"

"That's not important." Michael shifted. "We have video evidence showing you leaving the bar about three minutes after Flash Slivinski and Sarah Vance. Probably the perfect amount of time to follow them at a safe distance."

His cheeks turned a remarkable shade of red. "You don't know anything."

"We know that you work for Windsor Washington Golf Clubs and your company gave Flash one of his highest paid endorsement deals."

"That doesn't mean anything." Art raised his chin.

"We also know that you want to drop him from your line-up," Michael continued. "But doing so would probably cost you an arm and a leg. Considering business is already struggling . . . it seems like heads were going to roll."

Art glanced back at his teammates and called, "You guys go on without me. I'll catch up in a minute."

The men muttered something before turning back to the game.

Art shifted toward us. "I don't know what kind of game you're playing, but I didn't do anything."

"Then why did you follow Flash to the tavern that day?" I asked.

The question slipped out. I was probably supposed to stand by idly waiting for Michael to call all the shots. But the man was obviously lying. His eyes had shifted. His lip had twitched. His breathing had changed.

"I was there because I was trying to talk to Flash," Art finally admitted. "I needed to convince him to let us out of that contract."

"When he said no, you followed him and, in the heat of the moment, killed his date?" Michael said.

His cheeks reddened again. "No! It was nothing like that. You have no idea what you're talking about."

"But you did follow him?" I asked.

"I thought about it. Then I realized how desperate it would look. So I changed my mind. I figured I would try again another day. Turns out that when Flash killed the woman, he was in breach of contract. Problem solved." Art shrugged. "But I didn't do it."

"I guess that worked out in your favor, didn't it? With all this bad press, I'm sure you guys won't be penalized for breaking your deal." Michael didn't mince any words.

Art's nostrils flared, though the rest of his body remained calm. "I can prove that I wasn't there that night. In fact, I left that club and met up with some friends at a different club down the street. I'll give you their names and numbers, and they'll tell you that I got there well before that woman died, and I stayed until 3:00 a.m. when the place closed."

"I would like those numbers, if you wouldn't mind," Michael said.

Art pulled a pad of paper and a pencil from his front pocket and began jotting them down. Then, with a flourish, he ripped the sheet off and smacked it into Michael's outstretched hand. "There. Call them."

Michael glanced at it before turning his piercing gaze back to Art. "Before you go, is there anybody else you can think of who might have a grudge against Flash?"

My laid-back coworker was relentless. I was kind of impressed.

Art's eyes lit, as if the question excited him. "Believe it or not, there is. I would talk to his manager, Bernard Sutherland."

This was the second time the man's name had come up.

"Why is that?" Michael asked.

"Because I heard the two of them hadn't been getting along lately. And Bernard has a temper. If Flash found himself in the wrong place at the wrong time . . . there may have been collateral damage."

"Thanks so much for your help," Michael said.

We waited until Art was gone, following his friends. Then Michael turned to me. "That last question is always important."

"The open-ended one about who else might have done the crime?"

"That's when people always open up and say what they've really been thinking the whole time you've been talking to them. I never close out a conversation without it."

"Noted. Now what?"

Michael grabbed his bag from the bench, and we started toward Oscar's car. "Now we need to track down Flash's manager and see what he has to say."

CHAPTER SEVENTEEN

As soon as we reached Oscar's BMW, I spotted something on the window. A paper.

I started to grab it, but Michael stopped me.

"Allow me," he said. "Fingerprints and all."

He grabbed a tissue from the glove compartment before picking up the corner of the paper. I read over his shoulder.

Back off or you'll regret it.

I sucked in a breath. That was a definite threat.

Whoever the killer was, he'd seen us here today. He'd left this note.

"This pretty much eliminates Art," Michael muttered. "He didn't have a chance to leave this."

"True . . ."

I glanced around. There was that feeling. The feeling that somebody was watching me.

The strange thing was I'd begun to sense that well before

I'd taken this job. I wanted to believe the feeling was somehow tied in with my current case. But what sense would that make? My gut feeling told me it could possibly tie in with my father.

I looked back at the note. The uneven script was hard to read, like someone had written it quickly. Based on the thin strip of plastic at the top, the paper had been pulled from a pad.

"I'll see if I can find anything on this, but I'm not holding my breath," Michael said. "And that's a true fact."

"True facts are better than fake ones, that's for sure."

Humor glimmered in his gaze. "Come on. Let's go."

An uneasy feeling seized me as I climbed into the car.

"Do me a favor," Michael said as we started down the road. "Call Velma. Ask her to do a check on Bernard. I want to verify his alibi, especially now that it appears Art is innocent. I also want to know where he is now."

I did as he asked and then held my phone in my lap, running everything through in my mind. The feeling that I was being followed. The facts of this case. My dad's journal.

Especially my dad's journal.

Finding it had shaken my world.

"What are you thinking?" Michael asked. "You look pale."

I pushed away my thoughts and turned to Michael. The last thing I wanted to do right now was to explain myself, to voice my concerns aloud.

Yet, I did. It would be so nice to have somebody to talk to. Tahlia was still in Yerba, and I didn't get to speak to her that much anymore. My secret concerning my father almost felt like a burden.

I couldn't just share it with anybody. If my dad was really a spy, then that fact was top-secret.

I shoved the thought back down deep inside me again and tried to forget about my discovery for the time being.

"I guess I'm just trying to process everything that's been happening," I finally said.

"I know it can be a lot. But you'll learn the ropes."

"You just seem so good at this." I meant the words. Michael was a natural when it came to making up stories and talking to people.

"According to my parents, I've always been a talker. It's my gift, I suppose."

"I can see where that gifting really comes in handy." I paused and pulled in a deep breath, glancing over my shoulder one more time. "Do you believe him?"

"Who? Art?"

"Yes."

"He had all the signs that he was telling the truth, but I'll verify."

"Seems like a good idea. So now we try to talk to Bernard, huh?"

"It seems like a logical progression."

"And we just keep doing this until we turn over some information that might prove that Flash is actually innocent?"

Michael shrugged. "That's usually the way it works. We need to try to get these charges dropped."

"And if he is guilty? What do we do then?"

"Then we'll let the evidence do the talking. This is the difference in what we do and police work. In police work, you try to find the truth. In our line of work, you try to prove that the client is innocent."

"I see." I rubbed my throat again, suddenly feeling uncomfortable.

"When we get back to the office, I'm going to write this information down so we don't forget. I'll also make some follow-up phone calls to make sure Art really went to that other club during the time Sarah was murdered. Then we can try to locate Bernard."

"It sounds like we have a plan."

We parked in front of Driscoll and Associates and walked toward the front door. As soon as I stepped inside, I spotted a man talking to Oscar outside his office.

I'd never met the man before, but it didn't matter.

I knew who he was.

Flash Slivinski.

He was here at Driscoll and Associates.

And he looked angry.

Oscar turned to Michael and me as soon as we stepped inside. Based on the simmering heat in his eyes, he was on edge. Had Flash caught him by surprise? Either way, I braced myself for whatever this conversation might hold.

"Elliot, I would like you to meet Flash Slivinski. Flash, this is Elliot, my newest hire. She saved my life last night so we decided to keep her on the team." Oscar let out a deep chuckle, one that seemed to indicate he wanted to keep Flash guessing as to whether or not his words were true.

I might laugh too if his words weren't so true. If I hadn't put my own life on the line, I would be out of a job right now. The thought wasn't comforting.

Flash looked different than I'd expected. The man was much smaller than I envisioned but seemed solid. His hair was blond but thinning, his complexion ruddy, and his motions quick and confident.

"At least she gives you something pretty to look at around here." Flash gave me a once-over before looking away, no hint of apology in his gaze.

I wanted to growl beneath my breath. Michael touched my arm, as if he sensed my rising frustration. No wonder Flash had hired Oscar. The two seemed perfect together.

They were both jerks.

"Let's meet in my office and talk," Oscar said. "You too, Dor—Elliot."

I felt it again. That flutter of nerves that was becoming all too familiar. I had nothing to worry about, I reminded myself. I had met with dignitaries before, so I wasn't sure why this impromptu meeting had me feeling so off-balance. Maybe it was just because I was out of my comfort zone. Maybe proving myself was more important to me than I thought.

Velma gave me a compassionate look before we disappeared inside Oscar's office. Oscar took a seat behind his desk, while Flash sat in the lush chair in front of him. Michael and I took two foldouts in the corner.

"So, where do we stand with the case?" Flash asked, his motions quick and pushy. "I need evidence that I didn't do this, and I really hope the two of you found something."

Part of me wanted to forget everything I had already learned. Why should I help this man? He didn't represent anything I admired. I was sure when all this was over, it would be too much for him to even give me a thank you—if we managed to clear him.

What would my dad do? He'd work with all of his heart and mind and strength.

I knew that's what I needed to do also.

But I let Michael take the lead for now.

He ran through what we'd learned, starting with going to Flash's condo, leading into our visit to the club, and ending with our chat with Art today.

"Sounds like you've done a lot of work for nothing." Flash scowled and swiped some lint from his shirt.

"We're doing our best to uncover everything we can." Michael remained unaffected by his words.

"You need to work harder!" Flash slammed his hand on Oscar's desk so hard that even the pistachios jumped.

He clearly thought he had all the power right now—probably because he was the one paying us. But I still wasn't convinced Flash was an innocent man. No way was I going to let him make me feel inferior.

But I could still remain professional. That was one trait I had learned at my job in Yerba.

I drew in a deep breath before saying, "I want to ask you

about that camera we found in your condo. Any idea where it came from?"

"Not from me, if that's what you're asking." Flash narrowed his eyes, as if insulted by the question.

"You didn't have any secret recording devices around your house anywhere?" Michael asked.

"No." Flash leveled his gaze. "Anything else you need to know?"

"Actually, I was hoping to speak to your manager, Bernard, sometime today." Michael tilted his head, still as cool as a dewy mango in the morning. "Do you think there's any reason that he might have killed Sarah and framed you for it?"

"That's a good theory, but you're way off base." Flash shook his head so adamantly it was like an earthquake was happening inside of him. "Bernard was in Baltimore at a big soirée. You can check online. His alibi is solid. Besides, he wouldn't do that to me."

"You don't think there's any chance that he would . . . oh, I don't know, tell the police that you were a loose cannon?"

Flash's eyes narrowed. "Why would you ask that?"

"It's just a question," I said.

"Bernard would never do that to me." Flash leaned toward me. "Do you know something I don't?"

I kept my gaze level. "We're just exploring every possibility."

"I can tell you this," Flash said. "If you think I'm unpleasant, you need to meet Bernard. He's the one who made me this way."

I had some doubts about that, but I kept my mouth shut. Men weren't made this way. That was just an excuse. They allowed themselves to become unpleasant and rude jerks.

Flash stared at me, seeming to study my expression. "What else do you want to know? I want to hear more of what you're thinking."

"Well . . . since you asked," I started, rubbing my throat. "I'm confused about how you blacked out on the night of the murder. The tox screen came back clear."

"Except for some sleeping pills, but I take those every night. Why?"

"Were there elevated levels of the pills?" I continued.

"I didn't hear."

"Plus, it can take weeks to get definitive results like that back," Oscar added.

"Let's assume there were elevated levels of the drug in your system," I continued. "Maybe that could explain why you blacked out. Has the fact you take sleeping pills ever been mentioned in any interviews?"

His eyes narrowed. "You could say that. I did an endorsement deal with Naroquin. It's a sleeping pill."

My theory solidified in my mind. "So anybody could have known you took them . . ."

"I suppose. What are you getting at?"

"Let's say someone did drug you. Who might have done that?"

"Sarah would be the most obvious choice," Flash said.

"Did you guys have anything to drink when you got back to your condo?"

"Yeah, we had some wine."

"Where did you get it?"

Flash's face looked a little paler. "Bernard gave it to me."

I exchanged a glance with Oscar, who leaned back in his chair and nodded.

"If the police didn't take that bottle, we should have it tested," Michael suggested.

Flash continued to study my face. "You really think Bernard did this?"

I swallowed hard, contemplating how to respond. As I did, Oscar stared at me, something that looked close to a warning in his eyes. Did he expect me to say something that could get us fired?

This would be a good time to tap into some of that diplomacy I'd learned in my years of working for a politician.

"I don't know yet. I think you've made a lot of enemies," I started. "I think there are numerous people who may have set you up. At this point, I even feel like you could be guilty. But I don't have enough information to make a solid conclusion."

Flash stared at me a moment, and I fully expected him to unleash his wrath on me. Instead, he let out a deep chuckle.

"I like you. I like people who speak the truth. You've got a good one here, Oscar." With that, Flash rose from his seat and gave us one last glare. "Let me know what you guys find out."

He walked to the door.

I remembered Michael's earlier advice to me. "By the way, have you thought of anybody else who might want to make you look guilty?"

Flash didn't miss a beat. "The more I think about it, the more I'm certain there's only one person who could be behind this. Emily Riviera."

"Who is Emily Riviera?" I asked. That was a new name to me.

"My old girlfriend," Flash said. "All she cares about is money. She wanted to get married, but I saw the writing on the wall and called things off. She's never forgiven me for it."

"How long ago was that?" I asked.

"A year ago."

"Why would she wait so long to do something like this?" Michael asked.

"Beats me." He shrugged, the action brisk and hurried.

"Was Sarah the first girl you'd dated since Emily?" I asked.

Flash let out another deep chuckle, like that idea was preposterous. "Was Sarah the first girl I'd dated since then?" He let out another round of chuckles. "Of course not."

"Then why would Emily kill Sarah?" I asked. "Why not target someone else you dated in the interim?"

"Emily wasn't a suspect in my mind until a couple days ago. I ran into her best friend, a girl named Mischa Harrington. She started telling me that Emily has been obsessed with me since we broke up. She thought I was her ticket into the big time and that we were meant to be together."

"She told you that Emily said this recently?" I clarified.

"That's right."

I narrowed my eyes, trying to think this through. "But if

you went out with other women, what was so different about Sarah?"

"It wasn't Sarah," Flash explained. "It's the fact that Emily lost both her social status and her means. She's a manipulator. If Emily had the idea in her head that I was the solution to all her problems, she'd do whatever it took to get what she wants."

"So Sarah would have been an obstacle to Emily's plans," Michael said.

"Exactly. If Emily happened to see me out with Sarah, she may have had a fit of rage. She has a temper. In fact, I think she was arrested once for getting into a fight at a bar. She's a wild cat." He made his hand into a claw and slashed it through the air.

The action was really quite comical and showed me that this man wasn't as snobbish as I'd thought. There was still an awkward little boy hiding down deep inside him.

"You didn't think to tell us this sooner?" Michael's jaw hardened.

Flash let out a puff of air through his nose. "You have no idea how many enemies I have. If I started to tell you all of them now, we would be here all day."

I made a mental note of that to store away for later.

It seemed like everyone around here had enemies . . . including me.

CHAPTER EIGHTEEN

While Michael typed some notes about our conversation with Art, I sat at my desk eating my peanut butter sandwich and an apple and drinking my water. As I did, I researched Emily Riviera.

As soon as I typed her name into the search engine on my computer, gobs of results popped up. This was a woman who wanted to be known via social media. She wanted to be an influencer, if I had to guess. It seemed as if her whole life was laid out for anyone to see.

Normally, I wouldn't think being such an open book was wise—I certainly wouldn't advise my sister to do something like this. But, in this case, I figured Emily's oversharing about her life would work in our favor.

I scrolled through everything she'd recently posted. There were pictures of her with other men. Pictures of her with her best friend, Mischa. Pictures with Flash, complete with the caption of, "I'm so glad that we can be friends now. You're the best."

I paused. Emily had just posted that a couple weeks ago.

Was what Flash told us true? Did she still have a thing for him, and was she hoping they would get back together?

From pictures, she appeared to be the type who liked the clout that came with dating a celebrity. There was just something about the way she posed and flashed her smile that made it clear she ate up any attention she could get.

From what I could tell, she was twenty-four years old. She was petite and thin, with long, dark hair that was styled in perfect waves. Her cheekbones looked even and symmetrical, as did her eyes. But there seemed to be something missing when I looked at her gaze. A certain depth or compassion.

Those were all assumptions, of course.

I kept scanning her information. Apparently, Emily had worked retail for a while, and she'd also done some waitressing jobs. Now she was about to open her own clothing boutique.

It just happened to be here in Storm River.

I went back to her Facebook page, which was mostly public. Something there caught my eye. Tomorrow night, Emily was going to a fundraiser for an animal shelter at a local mansion in town. Tickets were a thousand bucks each, and there were still five left.

I tapped my finger on the desk for a minute. A thousand bucks each? It was insane. That would pay our rent and buy groceries.

But attending an event like that would also be a good opportunity to get to know Emily.

I glanced at Michael as he typed notes into his computer, and I took another bite of my sandwich.

If Oscar paid that much for us to go to this fundraiser, we had best not walk away without any answers. The pressure would definitely be on. Yet, at the same time, it seemed like our best chance of getting to know Emily.

I cleared my throat and presented my idea to Michael. "What do you think?"

He nodded slowly. "I think it's great. Let's go talk to him and see what he says."

The rest of the day had been a rush. Oscar had agreed that Michael and I should go to the fundraiser, and Oscar would foot the bill. But he also had some very stern warnings about the information we were supposed to find.

Oscar told us all of that while sipping a green smoothie and puckering his face as if it tasted like sewage. As soon as he was finished, he turned back to his TV and acted like we were dead to him.

This man really didn't do any of the work himself, did he? Here I thought I was going to be working for someone who was so great, and it turned out he was just a loser.

Yet, I still wanted to see this through. I wanted answers. Sarah Vance deserved some answers.

I spent the rest of the time in the office looking into

Bernard. Even though Velma had said he had an alibi for the night of the murder, I had my doubts. I'd studied all his social media posts—there were tons—from that evening.

No pictures were tagged during the time Sarah had died.

Would it have been possible for Bernard to leave Baltimore, come down to Storm River, and perpetrate the crime?

I did a few more calculations and leaned back. Based on everything I'd learned, the answer was yes. Definitely.

Where was the man now? Was he really working in Baltimore? Or could he be in town? For that matter, was he the one who'd left that note on the car windshield?

I had no idea.

I sighed and glanced at my watch. I had just enough time to go home and change into my standard cleaning outfit. Then I was off to the police station again.

I felt more nervous about tonight than I did on the first day.

The detective had already seen me twice. He'd almost caught me snooping through his file. If I messed up again, then I was sure to be caught and my cover completely blown.

I could do this. I *would* do this.

It wasn't because I didn't want to let Oscar down.

It was because I didn't want to let myself down.

CHAPTER NINETEEN

I frowned when I walked into the police station and spotted Detective Hunter at his desk.

His presence was going to make my job even harder. At least, when he wasn't there, I had a fighting chance of looking at his notes. But if he was sitting at his desk the whole time, there was no way I'd be able to see anything.

Tonight, I was back to my job of mopping again. I really hated mopping. It wasn't that I was above it, it just wasn't something that I enjoyed or found any satisfaction in. I'd rather be organizing or doing something where I could see notable changes. Mopping made me feel like I was pushing wet dirt from one side of the room to the other.

As I rinsed my mop, I thought about that name I'd seen in the file. Bernard Sutherland. Why had the man's name been in the file if he had a rock-solid alibi on the night of the murder?

My thoughts turned over as I squeezed dirty water into the bucket. What if his name was in the file because Bernard had been one of the witnesses saying Flash was guilty?

The thought made me freeze. I didn't know how to prove that, but if the man's name was in the folder there had to be a reason for it.

I knew that Flash had blacked out sometime between the time he and Sarah entered his condo and the time he'd woken up and found her dead. What happened in that block of time?

What if Flash wasn't telling the truth and he'd met Sarah before? What if it wasn't a romantic rendezvous at all? But, if not, what else would it be? I wasn't sure.

Still, the one thing that stumped me was motive. Aside from the physical evidence, the case just didn't make sense. *Why* would Flash murder Sarah, a woman who was supposedly a stranger?

I slopped my mop back onto the floor and continued cleaning. At one point, Detective Hunter looked up at me. His eyes met mine.

My first inclination was to stare back. But that would be a mistake—my character would be broken. Instead, I quickly looked away as if shy.

There was just no way I was getting information tonight. I needed to think harder. What would Michael do right now? Were there any tips he'd given me that I could tap into?

Maybe if I could just be invisible, I could find some answers.

I worked the rest of the room, saving the area near the

detective's desk until the end. Hunter sat there silently for the entire time I was in the room, studying a file.

There once was a girl named Sue. She didn't know what to do. But she tried to get nearer so she could see clearer, but she feared that she might spew.

I forced myself closer. As I did, another man walked up to Hunter. If I had to guess, the man worked in the lab. His white overcoat gave him away. Yes, I was astute. What could I say?

"The blood spatter analysis is back," the man started.

"And?"

"This is where it gets interesting. Look at the pattern here on the wall and on the carpet." He showed the detective some photos. "Now look at it on Sarah's shirt, as well as on Flash."

"What am I supposed to be seeing here? Can you give me the Cliff Notes version?"

"Of course." The tech straightened. "To be direct, it's quite clear someone left-handed is behind this crime."

Detective Hunter's eyes widened. "Are you sure?"

The lab tech nodded. "I am. Now that I'm looking more closely at the forensics, something about this investigation isn't adding up now. I re-created the scenes, complete with the blood spatter. I don't believe Flash Slivinski murdered Sarah Vance."

His words nearly stopped me in my tracks. If forensics had come back proving that our client may not be guilty, what did this mean about Flash's upcoming trial?

I didn't know. But at least I had something right now.

"Elle!" Rosa called. "*¡Vamonos!*"

I snapped back toward my boss, my cheeks flushing. Did she suspect I'd been eavesdropping? I had no idea.

I quickly gathered my supplies and made my way toward her. The crew met in a central area near the entry to the office area, and together we walked toward the lobby.

As we did, two uniformed officers—one of them Bradford —escorted a man inside. A big man. An angry man that reminded me of a snarling dog about to attack.

Just seeing him caused a shiver to race through me. I didn't know what he was being brought in for, but I definitely wouldn't want to encounter him alone in a dark alley.

Danger seemed to seep from the man like a contagious disease.

The cleaning crew stepped aside without being told. Each of us seemed to sense that this was no time to operate as usual.

The man muttered under his breath as the officers escorted him toward the booking area. As he passed, the man glanced at me. Something flashed in his eyes.

My lungs froze for a minute as I scooted closer to the wall.

I did not want this guy looking at me.

Especially not with that gleam in his eyes.

I waited for the men to move on, suddenly even more anxious to get out of here.

But just as the man walked by, his arms somehow broke free from their confines. He rose to full height like a monster rising from the mist.

The next instant, he lunged forward and grabbed me.

With lightning speed, he snatched an officer's gun from his holster and pressed it into my head.

"Everyone stand back or the girl dies!" he growled.

My head spun. Everything around me blurred.

What was happening?

Blood pumped through my veins with so much force that I thought I might pass out. Almost getting killed two nights in a row wasn't part of my job . . . right?

Yet, as I glanced around at everyone staring at me, I knew it *was* happening.

The monster-like man had a gun to my head.

Dear Lord, it's me again. Begging for your help. Pleading for your mercy.

Everyone around me froze as they stared, waiting to see what the man would do next. His actions seemed to shock the officers, who tensed and braced themselves as if unsure of their next move. No one had anticipated this.

Don't freeze, Elliot. Use that brain. Don't let this all be in vain.

I sucked in a breath, trying to gather myself. I needed to do what I did best. To observe. To make note of all the details around me—starting with the man who held me hostage.

I could smell him. Smell the fear and alcohol and cigarettes.

I felt his muscles as he gripped me. His thick skin seemed to indicate a hard life. His shoes were dirty, like he'd been outside.

This all wasn't going to end well, was it?

"I'm leaving with her, and, if anybody tries to get close, I will kill her," the man hissed, his spittle hitting my hair. "Don't test me."

I glanced across the room. Rosa stared at me with fear in her eyes.

They were probably all glad it was me, not them. I couldn't even blame them.

I gasped as the gun pressed harder, the metal digging into my skin.

Detective Hunter stepped out of the doorway, his hands in the air and his body language unassuming as he stepped toward the gunman.

"You don't want to do that," Hunter murmured. "Why don't you just let her go? She's innocent."

"I don't want to let her go. We're getting out of here." The man took a step backward toward the door, the gun still pressed to my temple.

Someone of his size and inebriation should *not* be walking backward with a gun. One wrong move, and his finger would hit that trigger, and I would be . . .

Needing a gravedigger?

This was not the time to rhyme.

I only knew I couldn't go out like this. Not at this place in my life. I was still finding my footing and forging a new way for myself. I felt like there was more I needed to accomplish.

"Just let her go and let's talk." Detective Hunter stepped closer.

How could he be so calm at a time like this? It was beyond

what I could fathom. But I was thankful for his presence. Something about his easygoing demeanor made me feel more at peace right now too.

He almost reminded me of . . . my dad. Papa had always been able to bring peace to tense situations.

I swallowed hard again.

"There's nothing that I want to talk about," the man said. "We're getting out of here."

He took another step back. I knew if I left this building with this man that I'd probably never be seen again. Gut instinct told me that.

I couldn't wait for someone else to save the day.

"Damien . . ." Hunter warned.

Damien? Did I recognize that name? I didn't think so.

I heard a click behind us and knew we were surrounded by officers. But could they really help me? I was at this man's mercy.

Even your breathing, Elliot. Keep a cool head.

It was useless. Adrenaline fueled my thoughts, my actions, my reactions.

The gun dug into my skin until my head throbbed and my mind swirled.

"You're not going to make it out of here alive." Detective Hunter stepped closer. "If you pull that trigger, then we will take you down. There's no happy ending here."

I wanted to frown at his words. The detective's statement had included me dying—and that wasn't a scenario I wanted to imagine.

Then again, the detective didn't think I spoke English, so I wasn't supposed to understand him. Don't look fearful but confused, I reminded myself.

"You don't want it to end like this," Hunter continued.

The man behind me froze. As he did, something about him caused a memory to rise in me. I'd smelled this man before.

I know it was weird, but I was certain of it.

My mind flashed back to the past few days. Why was this man familiar? I'd never seen his face before.

That's when it hit me.

This was the man I'd tackled in front of Oscar's office last night. I was nearly certain of it.

But what was he doing here now? Did he recognize me? Was that the spark I'd seen in his eyes?

Then I remembered the warning Jono had muttered after he'd helped me fix my car. *Be vigilant.* I remembered that feeling I was being followed.

Was this somehow connected? Had I been the target and not Oscar?

Nothing made sense.

If it came out that I'd tackled this guy at Oscar's office, I was going to have a lot of questions to answer. My cover would be blown.

My problems continued to mount.

I needed to think quickly.

Part of me thought I should be compliant, that it was the best way to stay alive.

But the other part of me told me that I should be feisty if I wanted to live.

What would my dad do?

The man shoved the gun into my skull even harder. I flinched.

My eyes went back to Detective Hunter. He still watched. Studied my face. Tried to assess the situation.

But I could feel the desperation from the gunman. He would pull the trigger. He didn't care if I was a victim here or not. I had a feeling that he didn't care if he was a victim either. He was drunk and desperate. Maybe he didn't even have anything to live for.

If that was true, then I really was in trouble.

Because he had no reason not to act. No motivation to stay alive.

"Just leave me alone!" the man yelled.

He was escalating. I felt his heart beating faster behind me. Felt the sweat coming off him. Even the way his chest rose and fell indicated that his breaths were becoming shorter and not as deep.

"Just put the gun down, Damien." Hunter's startling blue gaze returned to the gunman, and his motions were calm and steady.

Despite that, Damien was not putting the gun down.

There was only one thing I could think to do. And it was risky.

But if I was going to die, I was going to go down fighting.

Before the man could react, I raised my elbow and rammed it into his neck.

The motion took him off guard, and he reeled backward.

As he did, I swung my leg around and kicked his hand.

His gun flew through the air.

I grabbed his arm and twisted it behind him until he cried for mercy. Thank goodness, my dad had made me take years of self-defense classes. I just never thought I would use what I'd learned like this.

At once, cops surrounded Damien. One of them grabbed the man's gun.

The danger appeared to be over.

For now.

I collapsed on the floor and gasped for air as trembles claimed my body.

What had I just done? I wasn't sure.

But I did know that I was alive, and that was the important thing.

CHAPTER TWENTY

I was still trying to maintain my cover as I sat across the table from Detective Hunter in one of the interview rooms. He'd brought in another officer who spoke Spanish to interpret for me, and he'd gotten me the worst cup of coffee my taste buds had ever experienced.

I'd told Detective Hunter I'd never seen the man before.

It had been a lie. I didn't know what else to say. But guilt pounded at me. I knew I wouldn't sleep tonight because of it. I could feel the rock closing in on one side and the hard place on the other.

Maybe I would come back to the station later. Tell the truth.

I just didn't know anymore. Everything I'd ever prided myself in felt like it was crashing around me. My rigid moral compass now felt broken.

"It was very brave what you did, Elle." The detective leaned closer to me. "Kudos."

Once the detective learned that this man might be the same one who'd tried to shoot Oscar last night . . . would he and the other detective compare notes? Would they figure out that I was involved with both incidents?

Guilt—and a little panic—pounded harder at me.

The officer interpreted the detective's words. I glanced at Hunter and nodded, muttering, "Gracias."

Hunter leaned toward me, less hard-nosed professional and more compassionate problem solver. "You should learn some English. We could use more brave men and women at the station. You have good instincts."

I blushed before I could stop it. As the interpreter rattled off Hunter's statement, I looked away, afraid my gaze would reveal too much.

Finally, I muttered, "Gracias" again.

Hunter stared at me another moment before finally saying, "I need to get your number in case I have any more questions for you."

After Hunter's interpreter repeated his words back to me, I wrote my cell down on a piece of paper. I had to remind myself to answer any future unknown callers in Spanish.

A few minutes later, Officer Bradford was assigned to drive me back to my car at the motel. The rest of the cleaning crew had already gone. He'd blathered on and on as he drove, obviously loving the sound of his own voice since I wasn't supposed to understand his English.

I couldn't even pay attention. Instead, I soaked in his vehicle. Took notice of the fact he loved Mountain Dew—empty bottles of it were on the floor. And he apparently liked cats because a couple cartoon cards with the felines were shoved into a drink holder.

As soon as he'd dropped me off and I was alone in my vehicle, my muscles turned to Jell-O.

That had been a foolish thing I'd done tonight. But my life had flashed before my eyes.

The good news was that I'd ended up victorious. The thought made a whoosh of relief escape from me.

I wasn't sure whether to celebrate or cry. But victory and defeat seemed to clash inside me. Sure, the ordeal had been terrifying. But I'd also proven to myself that I was tougher than I thought.

I gripped my steering wheel.

I needed to get home. It was well past midnight, and I was sure that my mom was waiting up for me.

It was becoming harder and harder to explain to her why I was wearing khakis with a white shirt and smelled like Clorox every night. She was bound to start asking questions.

Despite that, I was ready to get home.

What a day.

Tomorrow was going to be another big day also. I had a fundraiser to attend—and answers to find.

"I know what you're hiding from me." My mom wagged her finger in the air as she stared me down.

She assaulted me with the statement as I stepped through the front door. I tried to keep my face placid as I deposited my purse on a table near the foyer. But heat already rose up my neck toward my cheeks.

How had she figured it out?

I swallowed hard before asking, "What makes you think I'm hiding something from you?"

Deflection. It seemed like a good method right now.

Her face tightened. "Don't lie to me, Elliot. Something hasn't been right this week, and I just now figured out what."

I sucked in a long, low breath and waited for her to continue. "What's up?"

"When you said that you were hired at that law firm, you didn't tell me that you were hired to *clean* for them."

Realization washed through me. Her conclusion made perfect sense. But my secret was still safe.

I licked my lips, trying to figure out how to respond. "Mama . . ."

"Don't *Mama* me. You didn't get all your education and all your smarts just to end up working as a cleaner. Not that cleaning isn't honorable, but you're wasting your talents and abilities if that's what you're doing."

"It's not like that."

"Then you better start explaining to me what exactly it is like." Her stare burned into me.

I let out a sigh and wondered how I was going to get out of this one. It was one thing to lie to the police, but it was a whole entirely different story to lie to my mom.

I needed to stick as closely to the truth as possible. "I do work for Driscoll and Associates. But I was given the opportunity to get some extra work in the evenings. I knew we could use the money."

It wasn't the complete truth, but it wasn't a total falsehood either. I knew, deep inside, a lie was still a lie. But . . .

I was going to have a lot of amends to make sometime in the very near future.

Right now, I waited for her reaction, which seemed suspended as my words sank in.

My mom's face softened, and realization rolled over her features. She rubbed my arms. "Oh, Elliot. I had no idea. I am so sorry that I assumed the worst."

"It's okay."

"I hate to see you working so much. You look so tired."

I was exhausted. My head throbbed. My trembles came and went. "I'm still adjusting, but I'll be fine."

"Hopefully not much longer. I heard today that Ruth was number twenty-four on the transplant list." A hopeful smile drifted across her face.

"That's great news."

"We don't know how soon that will be." She wrung her hands together. "It could still be another year or it could be another month. I just know that we have to have the money in place before they will do the surgery."

"I am trying hard, Mama."

She rubbed my arms again. "Oh, I know you are, sweetie. I know you are. Why don't you go get some rest? You look like you could use it."

I pushed down my guilt as I walked past her. I hated myself for not telling her the truth.

But I also couldn't wait to be by myself. I needed to decompress, and I knew just the perfect way to do it.

By reading another entry from my father's journal.

After I relished a new entry from my father, I pulled out my laptop computer. I felt even more determined than ever to find answers.

I did a couple of quick searches, researching more on Sarah Vance, Flash Slivinski, and Bernard Sutherland.

Then I remembered the poster I'd seen inside the police station. The one offering the 100K reward for information leading to the arrest of the Beltway Killer.

My family could really use money like that. I knew it was foolish to think I might be capable of something like that, but . . . what if it wasn't?

Out of curiosity, I typed in "Beltway Killer" to my search bar. Pages and pages of results popped up.

The first murder had been three years ago. All the victims were female in their twenties. The killer's manner of death was strangulation.

The women had disappeared, not to be seen or heard from for weeks. Then, one day, their bodies had appeared in a public location.

The police had only one lead in the case—a postal carrier.

But he'd been cleared, and there were no other suspects listed in the articles I read.

I scanned the photos of his victims. The first was an African American woman with a bright smile. The second victim was a redhead. The third victim—

I paused.

Was that . . . ?

I squinted, looking closer.

It was.

This was the same woman I'd seen in the photo on Hunter's desk.

His wife or girlfriend had been one of the killer's victims.

The air left my lungs at the thought of it.

I couldn't even imagine what that might be like.

I glanced at her name. Kate Snelling.

They hadn't been married.

My curiosity about the detective grew even larger now that I knew what he'd been through. No wonder he always had that intense look in his eyes.

CHAPTER TWENTY-ONE

*R*uth and I talked over a breakfast of fruit and yogurt the next morning. As we did, all I could think about were my father's words that I'd read last night.

I stuck with my plan to just read one journal entry per day to keep me going for now. That way I could spread all of this out and feel like I was reconnecting with my father even though he was no longer here on this earth.

Smarts will keep you alive. Integrity will keep you sane.

Words of wisdom from my dad.

"Have a great day, Sis." Ruth leaned forward and kissed my cheek. "Maybe this weekend we can catch up. Maybe we can make some popcorn and play Sapo?" It was our favorite South American game, one where you tossed coins and tried to get them into a frog's mouth.

I smiled and patted her hand. "I would love to do that. It sounds perfect."

"Then I'm going to put it on my calendar."

"You keep a calendar?" That didn't sound like my sister.

"No, but I'm trying to be more American."

We both exchanged a chuckle.

Ruth's smile faded, though. "I miss Papa, Elliot."

I reached across the table and squeezed her hand. "I miss him too."

"It just doesn't seem fair that he was taken from us so early. He was perfectly healthy one day and gone the next."

"I still expect to hear him coming home sometimes," I admitted. "I'd give anything to talk to him."

"Me too." Ruth rubbed beneath her eye. "I miss Yerba too. I never thought I'd say that. But I think just knowing that we can't go back . . . it makes me want to go even more. I just want to catch up with my friends. And I want fresh fruit. And to sleep in my bed and wake up hearing the sounds of the jungle."

"I've thought those exact same things. But we'll get through this. Together."

She offered a sad smile. "I know. Thanks. I'm so glad I have a sister to go through this with."

"Me too, Ruth. Me too."

A few minutes later, we were both out the door, and I was headed to my job.

As soon as I walked into Driscoll and Associates, the rest of the crew met me at the door.

"I heard what happened last night at the police station," Michael said. "Are you okay?"

"I can't believe that man put a gun to your head," Oscar said.

"Did you blow your cover in the process?" Velma asked.

I stepped back, feeling a bit overwhelmed at their care and concern.

"Give her space everybody." Michael raised his arms as if to push everyone back. "So let's start at the beginning. Are you okay?"

I rubbed my head, feeling a tremble rush through me as I thought about last night's events. It would be a long time before I could forget about that gun against my head. Flashes of the incident kept replaying in my mind, causing my muscles to pull taut with fear.

Then I remembered I was okay, and my breathing returned to normal.

"I'll be fine. It could've been much worse." I glanced at each of them. "How did you guys even know about what happened?"

"It was in the newspaper this morning," Velma said.

"They didn't have my picture, did they?" Horror raced through me at the thought. What if my mom saw it and found out the truth that way?

"No picture," Michael said. "But we put the pieces together. Especially when we read that one of the house-keeping staff helped take him down."

"You assumed it was me from that statement?" I didn't think that fit my reputation.

"It made sense." Velma widened her eyes and nodded. "Especially after what happened the night before when you saved Oscar. You're one of the bravest people I've ever met."

"I'm not really that brave."

"I got this for you." She extended her hand, a coffee mug there.

I took it from her and read the words. "I am woman. Hear me roar."

"You didn't have to."

She shrugged. "I found it two years ago, and I've just been waiting to find someone to give it to."

"I don't know what to say. Thank you."

She beamed. "You're welcome."

I turned to Oscar, desperate to take the attention off myself. "He's the same man who tried to shoot you. Did you see his picture? Did you recognize him?"

Oscar muttered something beneath his breath. "Yes, his picture was in the paper. Are you sure?"

"I'm positive. He had the same smell. The same feel. The same breathing. I'm a detail person."

"He's someone I put in jail about two years ago. But he just got out about a week ago. He vowed revenge on me, but I didn't know he was serious." Oscar ran a hand over his face.

"Apparently, he was," Michael said. "But that doesn't explain why he tried to kill Elliot. Was it just a matter of you being in the wrong place at the wrong time?"

As I replayed the scene in my head, I remembered seeing something change in the man's eyes right before he grabbed me. The flash of recognition.

"Seeing me brought back something in him," I said. "Damien must have remembered how I tackled him before he could shoot Oscar. It was like something barbaric rose in him, and he grabbed me."

"Unfortunate." Velma offered an overblown frown.

My gaze shot from Michael to Oscar. "What if he tells the police he recognized me?"

"Then, hopefully, the two detectives on the case won't compare notes," Oscar said. "We'll cross that bridge when we get there. Not to change the subject, but did you find out anything last night?"

I remembered what I'd heard the tech telling Hunter. But I hesitated before sharing it.

"Well?" Oscar practically tapped his foot as he waited.

"I did overhear that detective saying something." I repeated what I had learned about the blood spatter and the killer most likely being left-handed.

Oscar's eyes lit with satisfaction. "That is great news. *Magnifico!*"

"However . . . the detective didn't look convinced," I added, trying not to get his hopes up.

"It doesn't matter if the detective is convinced. If they have the evidence to prove Flash isn't guilty, then he's going to be a free man." A strange smile tugged at Oscar's lips.

"The ultimate way that we can prove that he's innocent is by finding the killer, though, right?" I asked. I thought about Sarah Vance. Her family still needed answers.

Oscar met my gaze. "Yes, you are correct. Flash seemed to like you. He wants you on this case. I suppose that's good news for us because, the more work we do for him, the more we get paid."

Money. Was that what this all boiled down to?

The love of money is the root of all evil. The longer I lived, the more I felt certain this Scripture was true.

"The fundraiser is tonight so maybe I'll find out something when I talk to Emily," I said. "I already told Rosa I needed—"

"Who's Rosa?" Oscar interrupted.

"My boss. With the cleaning crew." I stared at him until he nodded. "Anyway, I already told her I couldn't make it in tonight."

"Speaking of which." Velma held up a credit card and her eyes lit. "The two of us are going to go shopping."

"Shopping for what?" At least she hadn't said dumpster diving.

"Shopping for a new dress for you. We can't have you stick out like a sore thumb at this soirée tonight. We need to get you a dress and shoes and jewelry. We need to fix your hair and do your makeup. It's going to be an all-day thing."

"But wouldn't my time be better served by researching . . ."

Velma grabbed my arm. "Nope. It's already been decided. You and I are taking a day to get you all fixed up."

I exchanged a helpless glance with Michael, who shrugged.

I sighed. I knew what that meant.

It meant that I was doing this whether I liked it or not.

"So how did you ever end up working for Oscar?" I asked Velma as we walked between rows of dresses at a high-end boutique in Storm River.

The place smelled like expensive perfume, and the minimalist design seemed more like a roadshow closet than a shop for the wealthy. But I supposed this was the style they'd been looking for, and it meant nothing to me either way.

In our short amount of time together, I'd learned that Velma was frugal with her own money. But when it came to spending other people's? She was a World Champion Shopper.

She glanced at me and smiled. "Oscar actually helped me out of a very tough spot. When he offered me a job, I knew I couldn't turn it down. He's not the easiest man to work with, but I wish you knew him before he was like he is today."

Her statement was unexpected. "What did he used to be like?"

She began sorting through some dresses and holding several up to see if they met her approval. None did. Not yet.

"He was kind," she said. "Still a little rough around the edges, I suppose. But he was determined to make the world a better place. You know he used to be a cop, right?"

"I had no idea." I couldn't see the man in uniform. He was too lazy. Too out of shape. Too focused on money and status. Besides, why had an ex-cop run away and let his newbie assistant tackle a gunman outside his office?

"He was framed and let go. He never got over it. But he

was so good at what he did. I'm glad he didn't give up investigating altogether."

"Did he help you when he was a cop or when he was a PI?"

She continued to riffle through the designer dresses with the efficiency of a professional shopaholic. "When he was a cop. The early days of him being a PI, he was determined to prove himself. There were a lot of good times. But ever since the Ernesto case, things really went downhill . . ."

"That was the woman who killed her husband, correct?"

Velma frowned and nodded. "That's right. That case was really a life-changer, in more ways than one."

I wanted to ask why, but, before I could, she held up a dress. "This is it. It's perfect. I think you're going to look fantastic."

I eyed the outfit. "Doesn't it look too small?"

"No, this is going to look great on you. Michael's tongue is going to fall out of his mouth. Every man at the fundraiser's will, for that matter."

I shook my head. "I don't know about that."

She gave me a what-for look. "Girl, you might not think you've got a great body, but you've got just the right amount of skinny and curves. You just need to accentuate what you've got."

"I just prefer something more modest." I picked up a dress that had a flowy skirt and slightly fitted bodice with some flowers.

Velma snatched it from my hand and put it back on the rack. "Girlfriend, if I let you wear that, then you should put me on your enemy list. You won't be winning any points tonight if you don that outfit."

"It's perfectly respectable."

"If you're going to church. In the country. With your dead grandmother."

I tried not to roll my eyes, but I was slightly insulted. My style wasn't that bad . . . was it?

She thrust the red dress at me. "Now, try it on."

I stared at it and found my winning argument. "It's red. You warned me against wearing red dresses."

She flapped her hand in the air, blowing my concern off. "It's okay because Oscar won't see you."

We stared off for a moment until finally Velma won. I was going to try this dress on, and I was going to hate it. I'd do that and go from there.

I slipped into the dressing room to begin the torture.

CHAPTER TWENTY-TWO

Instead of trying the dress on right away, I sat down in a little chair and pulled out my phone. I'd been dying for a minute alone. It was an introvert thing. Sometimes, I even escaped to bathroom stalls for the same reason—because I was all peopled out.

I turned on my phone. Something was bugging me, and I wanted to check it out before not knowing killed me.

I quickly did a search of our suspects—I even included Art, just in case. But I also looked up Bernard and Emily. I studied the pictures.

Two of them were left-handed.

Two? What were the odds?

Bernard Sutherland was the first. It was obvious by the way he held his cups, his pen, microphones.

But so was Emily Riviera. She even made a big deal about it in a couple of her social media posts.

Could this be the evidence we'd been looking for? It wouldn't hold up in court, but it gave us direction as to where to keep looking.

"How's it going in there?" Velma called.

I put my phone away, knowing I'd need to change quickly. "Almost done!" I called, slipping out of my jeans.

"Guess what? I just got a phone call."

"Okay? And?"

"We just had a witness come forward saying they saw Emily and Flash together on the day before Sarah died. The two were arguing. Michael is going to talk to the witness now."

"That's great." It was. Emily needed to be more carefully examined. So did Bernard.

I finished putting the dress on and stepped out of the dressing room, sure I was going to be escorted out of this boutique purely for the crime of looking absolutely ridiculous.

I frowned as I turned toward Velma.

Her eyes widened, and I waited to see her head shake in agreement. She was going to think this was awful also.

"Oh, Elliot . . . you look gorgeous." She led me to a three-way mirror and stood me in front of the lights there. "You look like someone who could have any man you wanted."

"I am not that kind of girl. I've always been the smart one." I'd wanted to be applauded for my achievements more than my looks.

"Then who would've known you had this fox hiding down inside you?"

I had to admit when I looked into the mirror under these lights that I looked different here than in the dressing room. Sure, the red dress hugged my hips, but it wasn't as short as I'd thought.

The front came down in a V, but it wasn't as plunging as I'd assumed. The sleeveless style accentuated my toned arms —toned because of genetics, not working out.

"All we need to do is get the right shoes, fix that hair, do your makeup, and we're going to be golden. Or should I say red? Red hot?"

"You really think so?" Because I had a *lot* of doubts.

"Oh, I know so." She grinned and nodded like I was her biggest dumpster diving find of the day.

However, I still wasn't convinced.

One of the sales associates sauntered up to us and looked me up and down. "I don't know who your date is, but he's going to be a very happy man."

I really wished they would stop referring to Michael as my date. But, for the sake of ease, I didn't correct them.

I wondered if Michael was having to go through all of this for his tux, but I imagined he wasn't. Guys had it so easy sometimes.

"Okay, we'll take this and some shoes and maybe a nice necklace to go with it," Velma said. "Then we'll get you checked out of here, and we're going to grab some lunch. I know this place that has some great soups and salads. You are going to love it. After that, I'll do your hair and makeup. I'm just so happy to have another woman working at the office with me. Things are going to be so much more fun now."

I took one more glance at myself in the mirror. Was this really happening? This was the dress that I was going to wear?

My new life in America was so much different from what I'd left behind. Part of me was afraid I'd start liking it too much and forget the values I'd grown up with.

But just wearing the red dress once wouldn't hurt . . . would it?

I decided to avoid my mom's questions and get ready for the fundraiser at the office. It was just as well. Michael had run home to get dressed and see his daughter. He'd told me he'd meet me back here at 7:30.

A rush of nerves washed through me as I waited for him.

He'd also told me he'd been researching Bernard. The man was currently in Boston, and it seemed impossible to speak with him in person. Michael had also looked into several of Flash's competitors, but he couldn't find anything on them.

I glanced at the time on my phone again. It was 7:31. Was Michael one of those chronically late people? I didn't know him well enough to draw any conclusions.

I paced the office as I waited, trying to walk my nerves out. I hoped I didn't screw up tonight. I hoped I was somehow able to conceal my childhood in the jungle in favor of looking classy and refined.

It was going to be a big task, however. You could take the

girl out of the jungle, but could you take the jungle out of the girl?

I had my doubts.

Finally, my phone rang, and I saw that it was Michael. Quickly, I put the device to my ear. I hoped he was calling to say he was pulling up outside.

"Are you almost here?" I answered.

"Elliot, I am so sorry, but I can't make it tonight," he rushed, noise and chatter in the background. "Chloe broke her arm, and I've got to take her to the ER. My parents already have plans, and I can't leave this to a sitter."

His poor daughter. "Of course, you can't leave her right now. I totally understand. Take care of your daughter."

"I'm so sorry. I don't want to send you out there by yourself."

I remembered my father's words to me, his encouragement and his teaching. I could do this by myself if I was smart. It was what would keep me alive. Integrity would keep me sane.

I was still struggling with the balance of it all.

"I'll be fine. I'll stay invisible."

"Are you sure?" Michael asked. "Because I can tell Oscar that you can't make it."

"No, don't tell him that. Let me see how I do tonight by myself. If I need to get out, then I will."

"You can do this, Elliot," Michael said. "The only reason I hesitate to send you in alone is because you're new. I know you need a mentor. Maybe even more than one."

"If I'm cautious, I should be fine." I hoped. I liked to believe I could do anything I set my mind to.

"Okay then. Knock them dead. You're safer in crowds than you are alone. Always know your exits. And if you feel scared for your life, leave. Understand?"

"Got it."

"If you need anything, call me. I may not be able to come myself, but I will find someone who can help you."

"Got it. And tell Chloe I hope she feels better."

"I'll do that. Check in later, okay?"

"Got it."

I ended the call and felt a flutter of nerves and excitement rush through me. I could do this. I knew I could.

The question was, could I do this without getting myself killed?

CHAPTER TWENTY-THREE

Thirty minutes later, I pulled up to the waterside mansion and a valet approached my car. I wasn't the valet type. I was the one who'd rather walk one mile in the rain than pay five dollars to have someone else park my car.

Aside from that, I didn't really have the fancy fundraiser car that most of the people around me did. Mine was made in the US, and most of the others were foreign and looked more like trophies than vehicles. I really should have asked to borrow Oscar's . . .

Despite that, I knew I needed to keep my cover. Rolling my shoulders back, I embraced my new personality like a feather-clad actress at the Festival of the Chicken. I couldn't act like I was an assistant PI and part-time cleaning lady.

I shoved a twenty in the valet's hand as I climbed out of the vehicle holding my ten-dollar purse.

The irony. Would anyone besides me understand it?

Probably not.

Careful to balance myself in heels, I stepped away from the vehicle, straightened my little red dress, and started toward the massive mansion in the distance.

I had to admit that the number made me feel like a million bucks. As did having my hair fixed and my neck adorned with a gold necklace.

I'd never thought I was the type who'd like getting dressed up like a princess, but maybe inside every little girl, there was a bit of that fairytale fantasy hiding.

I drew in a deep breath as I climbed twenty-two steps to the front door. Yes, I counted.

The landscape and building around me looked neat and tidy, evidence that whoever had designed this place had been top-notch. I might like it here. I mean, I'd prefer to be alone with a book and a cup of coffee. But, if that wasn't an option, I would embrace this new side of me.

A brief flutter of nerves washed through me again. I knew nobody here. Most likely, I was going to be standing around by myself, trying to look like I blended in. Talking to strangers wasn't my number one favorite thing to do. But I could adjust.

I pulled my ticket from my purse and handed it to a man wearing a tuxedo in the doorway. He looked at it, glanced at me, and then extended his hand to welcome me inside.

I nearly stopped in my tracks when I saw the interior of the house. This place was massive.

Once, I'd been to the Yerbian president's house for an

event. Knowing my dad was a spy, the invitation now made more sense. Back then, I'd just figured that it was the luck of the draw that we'd been invited to one of the massive celebrations.

This place in Storm River almost put the Yerbian palace to shame. The mansion was gorgeous. The ceiling was at least three stories high. The floor appeared to be marble. A curved staircase stretched on one wall, and a massive crystal chandelier hung down in the center.

People dressed like a million bucks surrounded me. They mixed and mingled like they did this all the time.

Probably because they did.

This was going to be harder than I thought. Trying to blend in here. To look wealthy when I wasn't. To look like I was well-versed in the upper crust social scene.

What would people here think if they learned I'd spent my summer in the fields, picking gooseberries so I could earn some extra money for college. My dad had believed in personal responsibility. Nothing had ever been handed to me, and I'd worked for everything I had.

It gave me a great sense of appreciation for everything that I finally did have now.

As a waiter walked past with a tray full of bruschetta, I grabbed one and kept it on the napkin in my hand. Then I glanced around.

Where was Flash's ex-girlfriend? She was supposed to be here, and I needed to find her.

I moved toward the edge of the room to keep an eye on everything. It was something my father had taught me when he'd told me bedtime stories during the uprising. *Never stand with your back to the door. Always choose the best place to keep an eye on everybody.*

My gaze stopped at someone across the room.

Was that . . . Jono?

It was. He looked just as handsome and charming as ever as he talked to a group of ladies. He wore a tux, and his hair was perfectly styled. Was it as Michael had said? Jono liked to bring his flavor of the month to Storm River? To the house his father kept for him here?

Did the man even work or was he a trust fund baby?

My bets were on the trust fund part.

"Would you like a drink?" someone asked me.

I turned toward a woman wearing a black-and-white uniform, holding a tray of fluted glasses, and I smiled. The action seemed to catch her off guard because her gaze fluttered until finally a smile spread across her face also.

"Thank you." I took one of the glasses, knowing I wouldn't drink it but wanting to blend in.

She stared at me a moment. "You're welcome. And thank you."

"Thank me? For what?"

"For seeing me. Most of the time people look at me without even really seeing that I'm there. But you did. So I just wanted to say thank you."

I knew the feeling. Part of me wanted to tell her that I was just like her. But I couldn't break my cover.

"Excuse me, have we met before?" someone said behind me.

I swirled around and saw Jono standing there. Handsome Jono. Jono who'd muttered "be vigilant" to me. Maybe.

Who exactly was this man? A foe? A friend?

I had no idea.

I braced myself for how I should answer that question.

CHAPTER TWENTY-FOUR

"Have we met before?" I repeated the question as I tried to buy myself some time. "I don't think so."

I was so bad at this acting thing. *So* bad. But if I had to make myself do this, then certainly I could. My father had been a spy. He'd taken on alternate identities all the time. Certainly I could do the same.

Jono tilted his head. "No, I really feel like we've talked before. I just can't place when or where."

Would he buy that the girl he'd helped in the rundown, mostly silver except for the red door, Buick on the side of the road was now at this fundraiser that cost a thousand dollars a ticket? He would definitely find that suspicious. At least, if he had any sort of intelligence he would.

"I think I just have one of those faces," I said.

He still stared at me, almost as if he didn't believe me.

"Someone who's as pretty as you should be easy to remember."

My cheeks might have reddened. "Oh, stop."

"And you're not coy either. Where did you come from?"

I shrugged, really horrible at flirting. "I'm just an ordinary girl. What can I say?"

His eyes sparkled as they met mine. "I would say you're anything but ordinary."

And *that* was the reason people said this man had flavors of the month. He was good-looking *and* a sweet talker. He obviously wasn't all bad—he did stop to help women on the side of the road when their cars broke down.

"So what's your name?" His hand hung loosely in his pocket, almost like he was posing for a GQ picture.

Yes, I knew what the magazine was, even if I had grown up in the jungle. My old boss had liked to keep copies in our waiting room at the office.

I swallowed hard. "My friends call me Elle."

Not my friends. My dad. That was his nickname for me.

"Elle?" He grinned, showing his perfect teeth. "I like it. I'm Jono."

"Jono? What an interesting name."

He shrugged like it wasn't a big deal. "An interesting name for an interesting guy."

"You think of yourself as interesting?" It didn't seem like something most people said.

"Well, if I thought I was boring, then something would be wrong."

I couldn't help but chuckle at his words. The man *was* quite entertaining.

Someone across the room caught my eye.

That was her.

Flash's old girlfriend.

Jono seemed to follow my gaze. "Emily Riviera. Do you know her?"

I practiced my poker face, trying not to give anything away. "I can't say I do. I heard she dated that golfer, though."

"You mean Flash Slivinski?" There was no hidden hostility in his voice, but instead he almost sounded eager for some good gossip.

"Yes, he's the one."

Jono's gaze remained on Emily, but some of the sparkle left his gaze. "Yes, I do know Emily. Most of the people around here do."

"I don't hear a lot of fondness in your words."

"She's one of those who came from the wrong side of the tracks. But she's determined to marry herself into privilege."

Was there resentment in his words? I wasn't sure. "So you're saying she's a gold digger?"

He shrugged. "Yes. I suppose I was trying to be more eloquent."

"I can tell you are not a fan."

He frowned. "I have to admit that I dated her myself. But only for a month."

So everything that people had said about this guy *was* true. I didn't say that out loud though. Instead, I murmured,

"I guess I could learn a lot from you about the people around here, couldn't I?"

"I guess you could. Maybe we could get together for dinner one day?" His eyes glimmered as he waited for my answer.

I was about to respond when I glanced over Jono's shoulder and saw yet another familiar face. Who would've ever thought that I would recognize so many people?

But that was Detective Dylan Hunter.

Not only was he here, but he'd seen me talking to Jono.

In English.

CHAPTER TWENTY-FIVE

"Is everything okay?" Jono asked, studying my face, which had no doubt gone pale.

I scooted around so the detective couldn't see me. But when I smiled, I felt my nerves coming through.

It was crucial right now that I not break my cover. But I wasn't sure I was going to be successful.

I lowered my voice before responding to Jono's question about getting together for dinner one night. Under any other normal circumstance I would've told him no. But right now, I just needed to answer and I needed to answer quickly.

"That would be nice sometime."

His eyes lit with satisfaction. "Perfect. Can I get your number?"

I glanced over his shoulder and saw the detective coming my way. I quickly blurted my number, and Jono typed it into his cell phone. "Perfect. I'll be in touch."

Just as he said the words, Detective Hunter arrived, his gaze on me.

"Jono." He turned toward the man, nodding stiffly.

Jono nodded back just as stiffly. "Detective."

I realized the two of them knew each other but didn't have a fond relationship. This was not the time for me to ask about their history. But I was more curious than ever about the detective.

"I was wondering if I could have a word with your friend?" The detective's gaze went back to me.

"Elle?" Jono looked at me. "That's your call."

I shrugged. "Sure . . . I mean . . . sí."

I sucked in a quick breath. What had I just said? I fought the urge to close my eyes and shake my head at my stupidity.

"I'll call you sometime," Jono said.

I tried to remain calm and appear unassuming. But as the detective took my arm, I had to admit that I was a little more than nervous.

Michael had told me that I could call him if I needed anything.

I needed him now.

Too bad it was too late to grab my phone and make that call.

The detective led me away from the crowds and into a hallway.

This wasn't good. I knew what was coming, and I dreaded it.

"Who are you?" His eyes narrowed as he glared at me.

Suddenly, he didn't remind me so much of Captain America. Or maybe he did. I just never expected to be the one playing Red Skull.

Okay, so I had seen that movie. It was my sister's favorite, and I'd found myself enjoying it also.

How was I going to get out of this one?

I responded in Spanish. "Me llamo Elle—"

"Cut the act." His voice sounded hard and demanding. "I heard you speak English. Who are you?"

I swallowed hard. I wanted to just keep playing dumb. It was too bad that lying went against everything I believed in.

"I . . . do not . . . I no understand." I made sure my words sounded like broken English. Maybe this would work. But I knew desperation covered me like fleece on an alpaca.

"I know that you don't have an accent. I heard you. So stop playing games." He moved in closer, a classic intimidation tactic.

I felt my shoulders deflating. The man had me cornered. Plus, could I go to jail for lying to a police officer? But what if the police officer was off duty? Did it still count?

I had so many questions.

I stared straight ahead. Hunter's tuxedo bowtie was crooked. I wanted to reach up and straighten it.

I started to raise my hand but pulled it back down before I did something I'd regret.

But it seemed safer to stare at the detective's bowtie than it did to stare into his piercing gaze as he waited for my response.

"You do know that most liars have a response prepared, right?" Hunter said. "Taking this long to try to come up with some good story isn't doing you any favors. So I need you to tell me the truth."

Doggonit! He was right. I was taking entirely too long.

But maybe I could come up with an excuse as to why I was taking so long.

I squeezed my eyes shut and mentally shook my head. I needed to stop this. Now. I wasn't a game player.

"My name is Elliot Ransom, and I work for Oscar Driscoll," I blurted.

"What?" He stepped back and turned away, as if disgust filled him and he could no longer look at me. "Why would you work for that jerk?"

"I ask myself that sometimes too." I wanted to slap my hand over my face as the words left my lips. But it felt so good to be honest for once.

"So when you come in to clean the police station . . . ?" Understanding rolled through his gaze.

I nodded, knowing that he had already drawn the correct conclusion. "Oscar sent me to see if I could find out anything about your investigation into Flash Slivinski."

"Do you realize that what you're doing is totally unethical and illegal?"

"But—"

"I could arrest you right now." He stepped closer and lowered his voice, the action intimidating and threatening, just as it was supposed to be.

"I was just following instructions . . ."

"And pretending you didn't speak English?"

I didn't say anything. What else could I say?

"It was really quite brilliant," he said.

My eyes widened. Had I heard him correctly?

"I don't want to ever see you in the police station again," he said. "Do you understand?"

I nodded, probably a little too quickly. I needed to agree before he changed his mind. "I understand."

"If I see you there again, it's not only your job and future on the line, but the entire cleaning crew."

"They had nothing to do with this," I rushed.

"That's not the way it looks."

"But—"

"Look, you seem like a nice girl. A nice girl who probably got pulled into something that she didn't fully understand. So I'm going to let it pass this time. But if I were you, I'd run far away from Oscar Driscoll."

"Why?" I shouldn't have asked, but it was too late to take the word back.

"Because he's scum. He'll do whatever it takes to win. I know a lot of people think that's the way you need to operate in this business. But I don't agree."

The detective had scruples. I could admire that.

"Now tell me, what are you doing here?" He stared at me with a look that would send a cockroach scrambling back into its hole.

I wasn't a cockroach, even though I felt like one right now.

I knew there was no need to make up something at this point. I was cornered.

"I'm here to keep my eye on her." I nodded toward Emily.

Hunter followed my gaze. "That's what I figured."

"Because that's the reason you're here, isn't it?"

"That's none of your business." His stare was cold on me. "I can't make you leave this party, but you're swimming with sharks here. You should know that."

I rubbed my throat, suddenly feeling like I shouldn't be here. Actually, I'd known that all along. But his words only confirmed it.

"Good to know." My voice cracked as I said the words.

"And I'd stay away from Jono too while you're at it."

"Is there anyone that I *should* be around?"

"In this town? Not many." He looked back as Emily left the room with an unknown man. "I've got to go."

Before he could walk away, I called his name again and he paused.

"Just one thing," I said.

Hunter stared at me, waiting for me to say something.

But instead, I reached forward and straightened his bowtie. "There. All better now."

He narrowed his eyes, not in anger. But I was pretty sure I'd just perplexed him.

I was pretty good at doing that sometimes.

Then he walked away.

I released the breath I'd been holding. That was close. Too close.

But this night still wasn't done. I needed to see what I could find out about Emily. But it was going to be harder now than ever.

CHAPTER TWENTY-SIX

Another thirty minutes had passed, and I'd been wandering around the fundraiser aimlessly. This was not how I was supposed to be investigating. But everyone had clustered in groups.

Everyone but me.

I needed to come up with a plan if I wanted to talk to Emily. At this point, I was on borrowed time.

I paused near the staircase and spotted her across the room. I wasn't sure if Detective Hunter had talked to her or not, but she was back and talking to a group of friends. They each laughed as they stood in a semi-circle.

Here goes nothing.

I pretended to take a sip of my wine and made my way toward her. As soon as I approached the group, their smiles and laughter slipped, and they stared at me. I was obviously an unwelcome visitor in the space.

"This is a great event, isn't it?" I started.

They gave me stiff nods in return. Did they sense I wasn't one of their people? Or were they like this with all outsiders?

I had no idea. But if I had my way, I wouldn't be talking with them either.

"By the way, I love your dress." I turned to Emily and nodded at her Kelly-green strapless dress. It really was a head-turner. That hadn't been a lie.

"Thanks. Who are you?" The woman's voice was cold and direct, and her eyes assessed me as if I might be an enemy who'd sneaked over the border.

"I'm Elle. I'm new to this area."

"You have a beautiful skin tone," one of Emily's friends said.

I touched my face and smiled. "Thank you. The nice part about being half Hispanic and half Caucasian is that I always look like I have a suntan."

"I've always wished my skin was a little darker," another woman said.

Mischa. I recognized the painfully thin redhead from Emily's social media posts.

"I have to go have a fake spray tan done every couple weeks or I look like the walking dead," Mischa continued.

That sounded miserable. Her porcelain skin was beautiful, but I guess she couldn't see that.

I glanced around. "This place really is beautiful."

"Yes, my father likes it," Mischa said.

I glanced at the woman. "This is your place?"

I couldn't even begin to imagine having this kind of wealth.

"Yes, this is our place here in Storm River. I prefer our place up in Cape Cod more, but this works in a pinch."

Not only did she have one of these mega mansions, but she had two. Maybe even more. The facts surprisingly didn't make me feel inferior.

"So Storm River is a really interesting place," I started. "It seems dead during the week, but then on the weekends . . . it's party central."

No one said anything. Instead, they all stared. Had I just demonstrated party central by doing a brief rendition of the chicken dance? I was pretty sure I had.

Don't start rhyming. It would be awful timing.

Doh!

I cleared my throat, feeling my nerves getting the best of me. I had to get them under control before I blew it. "So, are all of you guys from this area?"

Three of the ladies nodded, but not Emily. Instead, she tucked a hair behind her ear and her eyes narrowed ever-so-slightly.

"I'm actually from New Jersey," she finally said.

"Oh? What brought you down here?" I tried to keep my voice light and friendly. And I really hoped I didn't break out in the chicken dance again.

"You like to ask a lot of questions, don't you?" She glared at me.

"I was making conversation. Don't feel like you have to answer. I'm just new in town, and I don't know anyone. It's . .

. different for me. My father was a diplomat, and, growing up, we had gatherings like this all the time."

The words were partially true, and I wondered if I seemed like someone with social standing if they'd accept me.

Emily stared at me for a minute before nodding. "I came down here for a waitressing job, if you must know."

I released my breath. Maybe I'd impressed her. Just a little, at least.

"But then she ended up dating Flash Slivinski," one of her friends piped in. "After that point, she was one of us."

"Flash Slivinski?" I made sure I looked totally impressed. "The one and only Flash Slivinski? Isn't he, like, the world's best pro golfer?"

I could tell that Emily was trying not to smile, but hints of it crept up on the edges of her lips. "That's right. But we're no longer together. He's out of my life now."

"That must have been quite exciting to date a professional athlete," I said. "I'm sure you had lots of events to go to together. You rubbed elbows with the rich and famous."

"I did get to meet Melania Trump one time. Regardless of your political affiliation, she is gorgeous, and she was kind."

"I can only imagine how fun that was." I nodded but tried not to overdo it. "If I were you, that would be totally all over Instagram."

This time Emily did smile. "Believe me, it was. In fact, I think I gained about ten thousand more followers that day."

"So awesome." My tone turned somber. "Hey, wasn't Flash accused of killing some girl recently? I don't always keep up with the news, but I thought I heard that somewhere."

Emily's smile disappeared. "That's right. We're all waiting to see what happens now."

"Do you think he did it?" I tried to look embarrassed by covering my mouth and raising my shoulders. "I guess I shouldn't ask that, should I? It just sounds like something from a movie."

"It's fine." Emily sighed. "We talk about it all the time because none of us can believe it. And I don't really know the answer. I did date the man, but I can't see him being violent. That said, he'd do anything to protect his reputation."

Now that was an interesting statement. "What is he trying to protect exactly? Did he do something wrong?"

"When you have that kind of money and fame, you feel like you can do anything you want and get away with it," Mischa added.

"It sounds like you *do* think he's guilty."

"I'm not saying that." Emily laughed as if I'd totally misunderstood her. "I'm just saying that you might be surprised at what people are capable of."

I glanced back at Emily. "I'm sure that you're grateful that nobody pointed the finger at you too, right?"

Apparently, I'd said the wrong thing because her friends' mouths dropped open and they stared at me in horror. I wished I *had* done the chicken dance again instead of saying what I had.

I swallowed hard before saying, "I mean, you know how it goes with people talking about jealous ex-girlfriends.

They're always suspect in cases like these, just like the jealous ex-boyfriends and spouses, right?"

"I'm just thankful that the police went straight to Flash on this one." A new hardness entered Emily's voice as she glared at me. "Now, if you'll excuse me, we need to get back to talking about stuff that . . . only we talk about."

I knew what that meant. She wanted me to go away. But had I found out any more answers just now? Not really.

That wasn't going to be good enough.

I needed to think of a way to talk to her more. My brain raced through the possibilities, and I knew I was going to have to take drastic steps.

The 65 percent of me that was introverted said no. But the 35 percent that was extroverted said go for it.

I didn't want to do it, but there was only one thing that I could think of.

As I turned to take a step away, my foot caught on the rug. I lunged forward, and my wine flew all over Emily's dress.

I gasped in fake horror.

"Oh, I'm so sorry," I said. "My toe just got caught . . ."

Her entire body tensed with rage as her mouth dropped open. "Look what you've done."

You would think I'd just ruined her whole life.

"I know just the solution to get that out of your dress," I rushed.

CHAPTER TWENTY-SEVEN

efore Emily could stop me, I took her arm and led her to a hallway I'd seen earlier. Just as we disappeared into the space, I glanced over my shoulder.

Detective Hunter stared at me from across the room, making no secret of the fact that he was watching my every move. The good news was that I wasn't doing anything illegal.

I didn't think so, at least.

I wished I could say I was surprised that he was keeping an eye on me, but I wasn't. I'd figured the man would be suspicious of me after discovering my real identity earlier.

As soon as we entered the bathroom, I grabbed a towel and put some cold water on it. I began dabbing the hem of Emily's dress where the stain had settled.

I felt her chilling gaze on me as I worked.

"Who *are* you?" Only her lips moved, while her teeth remained gritted.

Everyone seemed to see through me today. I needed to keep up my façade in front of Emily for as long as I could.

"I'm Elle. I just moved here."

"Why are you asking questions about Flash?"

"Can't a girl just be curious?" Tension snaked up my back as I waited for her response.

"He didn't kill that girl he was with, if that's what you're asking."

"Do you have any theories about who might have?" I dabbed the wine stain again.

She let out a slow breath. "I don't say this out loud very often, but Flash has enemies."

"Are you one of those enemies?"

Her lips formed a perfect O in horror. "Why would you ask that?"

"I heard you argued with him on the day before Sarah Vance died."

"Sure, we argued. That doesn't mean I killed anyone."

"Then tell me about these enemies of his," I countered.

Emily let out a dramatic sigh and rolled her eyes before looking back at me. "One night, Flash had been drinking too much. He has a tendency to talk a lot with a little alcohol in his system. He told me something that was . . . that was awful. If the wrong person found out what he did . . . it could ruin him."

My heart pounded in my ears. Was this it? This information I'd been looking for? "What did he do that was so horrible?"

Even though we were alone, she glanced behind me before lowering her voice. "I can't tell you. It would look bad for Flash."

"What if I told you that the police were looking at you as a suspect?"

A moment of triumph flashed in her gaze, followed by a crash of fear. "I knew it! I saw you talking to Detective Hunter earlier. The two of you are working together, aren't you?"

I straightened, forgetting about getting the wine out of her dress, and shrugged. Maybe it was better if I let her think that right now. "I'm not at liberty to say."

"I had nothing to do with any of Flash's bad choices. The only reason I've been talking to Flash so much lately is because he's going to help me out with my new business venture."

"New business venture?" I questioned.

"I'm opening a new clothing boutique. Flash is helping to finance it."

And that was really the reason she was being so nice.

"He's only helping you in return for your silence, isn't he?" It made sense now. "Why should we believe that you really are innocent?"

"Because I am!" She grabbed the towel from my hand and threw it at the mirror in a fit of anger.

I released the air from my lungs before saying, "Why don't you just tell me what happened?"

Her eyes narrowed as she stared at me. "Why should I?"

"If you don't watch out for yourself, who else will? Do you think Flash is going to defend you if somebody accuses you of murdering that girl?"

"But Flash is the one who's been charged with the crime!"

"Some evidence has come to light that makes it look like somebody else may have been involved in Sarah Vance's murder."

"It wasn't me!" Emily's voice rose as her eyes widened.

"Tell me what happened, Emily."

Even though there was no one else around, she stepped closer. "Fine. About three months ago, Flash was out partying and he had too much to drink. On the way home, he hit a car. Instead of stopping to see if the driver was okay, Flash took off. The driver was in ICU for three weeks and couldn't remember anything about the accident. He's doing okay now and all. But if the truth about what happened that night slipped out? It would ruin Flash's whole career."

Yes, it would. "Flash told you all of this?"

Emily nodded. "Like I said, it was only because he'd had too much to drink and he had loose lips. But when Flash realized what he'd done, he panicked. Flipped out. I told him I wouldn't tell anyone . . . that we could come up with a mutually beneficial deal."

"So you were really doing him a favor?" I didn't believe the words, but I said them anyway, just to see how Emily would react and to make her think that I was on her side.

"That's right. And that's all I know. Please don't tell Flash I told you that. I mean, if the man had died, it would be a different story. I would've had no choice but to come forward. But the man is doing okay. Flash made an anonymous donation to the man's medical care. He tried to make things right."

But that still didn't mean Flash had done the right thing. I kept the thought quiet. "Thanks for opening up to me."

Emily took a step back. "I'll figure out how to get this wine out of my dress myself."

That was fine with me. I'd gotten all the information from her that I needed.

I stepped out the door and back into the fundraising gala.

As the saying went, the plot had thickened.

I had gotten what I came here for. And now I really wanted to talk to someone about what I'd learned. Maybe I could call Michael, tell him, and he could get a head start on doing some investigating—provided that Chloe was doing okay, of course.

I glanced around. Nobody was watching me. They were all huddled back into their friend groups—friend groups like the ones I used to have. Would I ever find my place again?

I wasn't sure.

With that in mind, I started toward the back of the mansion. I knew from my brief perusal when I'd felt socially ostracized that there was a patio out there. I'd been remembering Michael's advice to me: always know your exits.

I hoped there might be somewhere private I could call

Michael with an update. But that might go against his other advice: I was safer in crowds.

I didn't want to mess this up. But I thought I was done here, that I'd gotten the information I came for.

Just as I thought, a few people were out here mingling, but the majority of guests were inside. I pulled my phone from my little purse and walked to the edge of the patio, just out of sight so nobody would overhear anything I said.

I dialed Michael's number, and he answered on the first ring. Concern laced his voice before I'd even said a word. "Elliot. Are you okay?"

"I'm fine. How's Chloe?"

"She just got her cast put on, and we're waiting for the doctors to discharge us. Overall, she's doing fine."

"I'm glad to hear that. I know things like that can be traumatic for a kid." I looked around. Beyond the house, all I could see were shadows and the vague outline of a guest house. I knew the river stretched in the distance, though I couldn't see it.

I realized how isolated I was and shivered.

Maybe coming out here was a bad idea. Privacy equaled isolation, which presented opportunities for bad things to happen.

"I appreciate you asking," Michael said. "But what's going on there? Like I said, I'm really sorry that I wasn't able to be there to help you."

I told him about the conversation I'd just had with Emily.

He let out a low whistle. "This could change things. I can't believe Flash was involved in a hit-and-run. Actually, I can."

"If this Sarah woman somehow knew about that hit-and-run, maybe she brought it up, and maybe Flash really did kill her."

"But what about the information you heard about the crime scene? If Flash is right-handed and the killer was left-handed . . . something doesn't add up."

"I know. I've been thinking about that. So I did some research, and it turns out that his manager, Bernard, could have made it back to Flash's condo in time for the crime.

"But he was in Baltimore."

"It's less than a two-hour drive from Baltimore to this area. What if Flash suspected Sarah was going to try to blackmail him? Maybe he called Bernard, who told him to keep her occupied until he could get there. He could've done the dirty work."

"Wait, are you saying that Bernard is left-handed?"

"I thought I'd mentioned that to you earlier. Sorry." I glanced around again, suddenly anxious to get inside. I felt entirely too isolated out here right now. "That's exactly what I'm saying."

"You're doing good work, Elliot. But maybe you should get out of there now. I don't want to put you in a place where you're in danger. You've already had enough of that."

"I think I'm ready to go. I just wanted to tell you what I've learned and make sure I was okay to leave."

"I'd definitely say you are. Oscar will be pleased that he got his money's worth. I'll try to come in tomorrow morning so we can talk about our next steps. Okay?"

"That sounds good. Thanks, Michael."

I didn't realize just how much I missed having him with me tonight. The brief few days that I'd been working this job, I'd learned to depend on Michael's wisdom and advice.

Just as I ended my call, I heard a step behind me.

Before I could turn to see who it was, an arm snaked around me and something sharp pressed into my throat. A deep voice said, "Don't say a word."

CHAPTER TWENTY-EIGHT

I froze. Having a gun thrust into my skull was one thing. But feeling the prick of a knife against my skin was a whole different level of scary.

Whoever was behind me, I couldn't see his face. It wasn't Emily. I was sure about that.

But this man was left-handed, based on how he held the knife.

I felt the blood drain from my face at the realization.

The man nudged me into the shadows and out of sight of anybody who might be close by. The darker it grew around me, the more my hope faded.

Quickly, I glanced down. I saw his shoes.

They weren't a dressy type that someone would wear to an event like this. Instead, they were black loafers. He also wore dark jeans.

I could rule out Jono or Hunter—not that they'd been suspects.

Details helped me stay focused. Maybe they would even save my life. I just needed to pick up on the right details.

A wave of fear crashed over me, making my head spin.

"What do you want from me?" My voice cracked as I asked the question.

"I need you to drop this investigation."

"Why would I do that?" *Stupid question, Elliot.*

"Because you don't want to end up like Sarah Vance," the man growled.

My blood went cold at his words. No, I did not want to end up like Sarah. Was this what her final moments were like?

"How did you find me here?" My voice trembled.

"I know what you're up to. I've been watching you. You're getting too close."

"I can only assume you're the person who really killed Sarah Vance. But Flash has been charged with this crime. Why are you risking exposing yourself?"

"Because there's somebody else involved. Someone who needs to be caught before he acts again."

I froze, trying to let his words sink in. "What? What do you mean?"

"I mean, you're looking in the wrong direction. The real bad guy is still out there."

"Are you saying you didn't kill Sarah Vance?"

The man said nothing for a moment before blurting. "Flash

Slivinski is the most amazing golfer to ever walk this earth. I can't let him go to jail for a crime he didn't commit. But I can't let someone ruin him either, and that's what is going to happen."

I glanced around, looking for a way out of this. I saw nothing but shadows.

The thought made my head spin.

"It sounds like we're on the same side." My voice trembled. "I'm trying to prove he's innocent also."

He said nothing.

"Did you kill Sarah Vance?" I finally asked.

He still remained quiet. I could only hear his breathing in my ear. I took that as a yes.

"You killed Sarah because she was a threat. She was planning to expose Flash," I finally said. "And you were protecting him when you eliminated Sarah."

"Exactly." Understanding—and maybe relief—rolled through his voice. "I had to stop her. But I never intended for Flash to be blamed. I just didn't know how to fix it. I didn't have enough time. So I did the cowardly thing. I ran. And now it's too late."

"You could step forward and admit that you're guilty."

"But if I did that, I'd expose Flash for . . ."

"The hit-and-run," I finished.

"Exactly. I can't do that. I don't know what to do." Frustration rose in his voice.

I needed to talk this man down from the ledge before he did something he'd regret. Maybe I could even convince him to confess, let him know that was the right thing.

As the thought raced through my head, the man pressed the knife harder into my skin.

I wasn't out of danger. Not yet.

I swallowed hard, sweat spreading across my skin. "That doesn't explain what you're doing here tonight."

I heard people murmuring in the background.

If I screamed, would help come?

Most likely, it would be too late. All he had to do was move his arm and my throat would be—

I flinched. I couldn't finish the thought.

Though I'd had a moment of bravado last night, this situation was different. Death seemed closer. I was more isolated.

Plus, last night, my instincts had told me that I was going to be okay if I took matters into my own hands.

My instincts right now told me that my life would be over if I made any sudden moves. If this man had killed Sarah, he wouldn't hesitate to kill me too.

This man had found me out here. I was a definite target.

Last night, I'd happened to be in the wrong place at the wrong time, and I'd triggered that man who wanted revenge on Oscar. This was different.

I wasn't sure this man wanted to kill me. He wanted to scare me, though. Maybe he even wanted someone to talk to.

"Sarah was working with someone," he said. "Find him. And remember, Flash paid the medical bills of that man he hit. Flash made amends. He doesn't deserve this. None of this was supposed to work out this way."

What did that mean? Did Flash truly not have anything to do with Sarah's death?

Before I could say anything else, someone yelled, "Hey!"

The person behind me turned toward the sound. As he did, I glanced back.

Detective Hunter sprinted toward us.

As soon as the killer saw him, he released me and took off at a run.

Detective Hunter went after him, only pausing beside me for a moment. "Are you okay?"

I touched my throat, still feeling the prick of the knife there. It had barely cut me. "I'm fine. Go get him."

The detective raced after him. I prayed Hunter would be able to catch this man, despite his head start.

Until then, all I could do was wait and thank God I was alive.

Five minutes later, Detective Hunter returned alone, rubbing his head.

I didn't know what happened, but it didn't look good.

"He got away," he announced with a scowl. He slid his phone back into his pocket. "He had a car waiting in the distance, but I couldn't make out the plates. Backup is on their way."

"Are you okay?" I stared at him as he continued to rub his head.

He pulled his hand down as if the action had been at a subconscious level. "Yes, I'm fine. The man was hiding behind the carriage house, and he hit me over the head with something. It's the only way he was able to get away. The good news is that his arm hit something back there, and he cut himself. It will make him easier to identify later. Maybe we'll even get a hit off his DNA."

I frowned as I looked at Hunter. His handsome face was pulled taut with anger, maybe even some pain. Yet he still remained upright and almost regal.

"Maybe you should have your head checked out," I said. "Those kind of injuries can be serious . . ."

"I'll be fine." He scowled. "Now, tell me what happened."

I shivered, trying to collect my thoughts. As I did, Hunter pulled off his jacket and placed it over my shoulders. The warmth instantly made me feel better—as did the soothing scent of pine.

I shared what had happened out here on the patio. At this point, I didn't need to hold things back. It would only draw this out and make it more painful.

"Why did that man track you down here?" Hunter studied my face carefully.

"He's panicking. He's afraid we're going to find him and turn him in. And, if we do, then he'll have to share what he knows about Flash."

"Which is . . . ?"

I sucked in a deep breath. I hated to break Emily's trust, but I had no choice except to share what my client had done. "Flash Slivinski was involved in a hit-and-run accident after he'd been drinking. Even though the victim didn't die, the man was injured and ended up in ICU. Somebody saw it happen and planned on holding that information over Flash's head in order to get money from him."

The detective's eyes widened. "Was that person Sarah Vance?"

"That's my best guess."

"So it makes sense that Flash killed Sarah. He does have motive."

"Not really. Because Flash isn't left-handed."

The detective tilted his head and stared at me. "How did you know the killer was left-handed?"

I realized I'd just given away some of the information I'd learned while eavesdropping at the police station. "Would you believe me if I said I observed that looking at the crime scene?"

"No." He crossed his arms.

"Besides, that man who accosted me tonight was too tall to be Flash."

"Then who do you think held that knife to your throat tonight?"

"My best guess right now is Bernard Sutherland."

"Bernard has an alibi."

I glanced around and saw that a crowd had gathered in the distance, watching us. Two security guards strode our way, so I knew I didn't have much time.

I needed to make this quick. "True. But if you look at the timeline, you'll realize that Bernard could have gotten here from Baltimore just in time to do the deed."

Hunter blinked, almost like my words surprised him.

"But what sense would that make? Why would he want to set up his client?"

"He did testify about his character, didn't he?"

Hunter narrowed his eyes again. "No comment."

I took that as a yes.

"You really should leave all of this to the police," Hunter said.

"A girl's got to make a living."

He stared at me another moment, saying nothing. But I felt like his eyes could see into my soul, and I braced myself for whatever thought he was forming.

I wondered what Hunter's life was like now. How hard it must have been when that woman from the photo with him had died at the hands of the Beltway Killer. How was he dealing with that loss?

Was that the reason why he seemed so distant, even to the people he worked with at the station? Or had the man always been like this?

"Isn't there something else that you could do?" he finally said. "Something that would keep you out of the kind of trouble that Oscar Driscoll is certain to get you in?"

"I did work insurance, but I was miserable. Miserable and safe or happy and in danger? It's a tough choice."

He gave me that silent stare again, the one I couldn't read. I couldn't tell if he thought I was an idiot or a potential comrade.

"I don't know what to tell you," he finally said. "I just don't want to see you get mixed up with this guy."

"I appreciate your concern. But shouldn't you be out there looking for this guy?"

"I already put out an APB. More units are coming here. And it looks like I need to talk to Emily Riviera."

I frowned.

"What's that look for?" Hunter stared at me.

"Apparently, in exchange for her silence, Flash is going to help finance her new boutique."

Hunter raked a hand through his hair. "The lengths these people will go to in order to get what they want never fails to astound me."

"I told her I wouldn't tell you." Guilt nagged at me.

"But you did."

I shrugged. "Honestly, all I want to do is the right thing. I just never thought it would be this difficult to figure out what the right thing was."

Shouldn't it be black-and-white? I felt like the answers should be clearer, but they weren't. Or maybe I just wasn't listening to the still, quiet voice in my head. Maybe I was becoming complacent, arriving at a place where truth and lies were adjacent.

There I went rhyming again . . .

"That's a question that we've all had to ask ourselves in this line of work at one point or another. I hope you're able to grapple with the question and find a solution you can live with."

"Me too." I swallowed hard, hating how attracted I felt to this man.

He nodded toward the distance. "I should go."

I took off his coat, immediately missing the warmth, and handed it back to him. "Thank you."

"No problem."

With that, Detective Hunter walked toward the security guards, flashed his badge, and began telling them what was going on.

A few minutes later, I headed to the valet to pick up my car. As I waited for it to pull up, I saw someone sitting in their vehicle in the driveway.

I sucked in a breath.

Was that Flash Slivinski? What was he doing here?

As soon as he saw me notice him, he zoomed away.

But the eerie feeling in my gut wouldn't leave.

What I really wanted was to go straight home. But I knew my mom would be waiting up for me, would see me in this outfit, and would ask entirely too many questions. With that in mind, I headed back to the office to change.

As I stood under the bright lights of the bathroom, my reflection caught my eyes.

For the first time in a long time, I had a light in my gaze. When we had moved here, then my dad had died, all my joy disappeared. I felt like life was just a matter of going through the motions.

Something about this job was stirring up something inside me—some kind of purpose, a reason to look forward to getting up every morning. Even though I had yet to figure out the moral implications of finding the answers in the situations, I had felt a new sense of purpose when it came to helping innocent people find answers.

Even if they were innocent people like Flash Slivinski, who might be innocent yet dirty at the same time.

I took off the earrings and the necklace, and I placed them back into the boxes they'd come in. Then I changed back into my favorite jeans and a black sweatshirt. I let my hair down from the clip that held it back and washed the makeup off my face.

The woman who stared back at me looked like a whole different person.

I *was* a whole different person now. As much as I wanted to hold on to parts of my old life, the hope was foolish. I was starting over again in the States. My life here would never be anything like it was in Yerba. The culture was different, and, like it or not, the culture was bound to change me in some ways.

The key was to not let it change me in negative ways. I could still be community minded and hospitable. I could still enjoy the simple things of life. I could still stop myself before I got caught up in this rat race.

But I could also embrace this new side of me. The side that operated in the fast lane, that was bolder and less subtle. My introvert meter might even move from 65 percent to 50 percent with a little work.

I could prove to my dad that I was more like him than we ever thought.

At my age, I thought I was beyond having to figure these

things out. But, apparently, I wasn't. I was starting over and having to rediscover myself.

I tucked my outfit in a bag that I stashed under my desk, sprayed myself with my Lysol so I'd smell like I'd been cleaning, and then I started home.

I needed to figure out when I was going to come clean to my mom.

But as I climbed into my car, that feeling filled me again.

The feeling of being watched.

I hit the locks on my car doors and glanced behind me.

I saw no one.

But I needed to get home.

Now.

Be vigilant.

Yes, I needed desperately to be on guard.

Now more than ever.

CHAPTER TWENTY-NINE

I hadn't been able to sleep much last night. I had too much on my mind. Mostly, I kept thinking about everything that happened at the fundraising gala. I remembered Emily's revelation. I remembered the man who'd put a knife to my throat. I remembered my conversation with Detective Hunter, and the dinner invitation from Jono.

As I lay in bed with early morning sunlight trickling in through my window, I kept going back to the man who'd cornered me last night.

Had it been Bernard? He seemed like an easy conclusion, but, based on the look Detective Hunter gave me, Bernard wasn't guilty. I didn't know what Hunter knew that I didn't, but my gut told me I needed to keep looking.

And then there was that note that had been left on the car windshield, warning us to drop the investigation.

The thing was . . . it was written by someone who was right-handed. That seemed clear based on the direction of the scrawl.

That meant that there were two people who'd been trying to scare us off this investigation: Sarah's killer and the person who'd been working with Sarah.

I closed my eyes. I needed to replay last night, detail by detail. My entire body tensed, and my breath came faster at the thought of it. I didn't want to recall the terror I'd felt.

But I had to.

Doing this was vital if I wanted to find answers.

The knife-wielding man's voice was somewhat familiar, I realized. I had a feeling he was trying to disguise it. That might mean that I'd heard it before and he would've realized that.

I remembered the words I'd read in my dad's journal last night. *Always keep your eyes wide open. Opportunities are everywhere. You just need to seek them out.*

That meant I would need to examine everybody I'd talked to since the start of this investigation, especially those who may not be obvious.

There was also a certain smell that the man had. But what was it? I wasn't sure I knew how to place it, but I'd definitely smelled the scent before. It was a mix of vanilla . . . and oak.

What sense did that make?

I felt like the answers were right on the edge of my consciousness, but I just couldn't quite reach them.

I sighed and leaned back in bed. Then I grabbed my laptop.

I had a couple things I wanted to research, including any connection between Bernard and Sarah.

When I finished, I knew I needed to go into the office to discuss everything that happened with Oscar and Michael. Maybe between the three of us, we could figure out something.

I was going to have to tell Oscar about Flash's hit-and-run. I'd also need to admit that I'd told the police that information.

No one should be above the law.

Finally, I got out of bed and got dressed.

When I walked into the kitchen, my mom and sister were already at the table. It was Saturday, so my mom didn't work today. But Ruth was already dressed like she might go somewhere.

"Something about you looks different today." My sister shifted at the table, her elbows resting in front of her, and her gaze curious.

I touched my face, wondering if I had forgotten to take off some of my makeup. I was pretty sure I hadn't, though. I remembered scrubbing it off at the office. Anything I missed should have come off in the shower.

"Maybe I just got a good night's sleep."

She narrowed her eyes. "No, it's a bounce in your step. I knew I'd seen it before, but it's even more prominent today."

"Maybe she just likes her new job with Driscoll and Associates." My mom put a plate in front of me with *desayuno peruano*. It was a traditional Yerbian breakfast consisting of

French bread, pork chicharron, blood sausage, scrambled eggs, and fresh fruit.

The look my sister gave me made me a little nervous, but I quickly looked away and stabbed a piece of sausage instead.

"Thanks for cooking this, Mama." I lifted my fork. "It looks delicious."

"Don't forget to say your prayers," she reminded.

"I will." I closed my eyes and thanked God for His provisions. I also asked for His protection.

When I opened my eyes, my mom said, "I splurged and got some mango down at the market. It always makes me feel like home."

Even though my mom had spent twenty-two years of her life in the States, she considered Yerba her home country. And I couldn't blame her. I knew she'd had some wonderful years there with my dad.

She'd invested in that community. She'd helped take care of the children, offering food and soap and clothes, all while telling them about Jesus.

I wondered how much she really knew about my dad. I wanted to know if he'd told her about his career. But there was no way to find out that information without asking specifically. And if she didn't know . . . then I would be revealing a secret I didn't want to reveal.

"Are we still on for playing Sapo tonight?" my sister asked.

"Absolutely. I put it on my calendar." I winked at her, and she smiled. "What are you guys up to today?"

"I was offered an extra shift at the drugstore," Mama said.

"My friends and I are going to go hang out down at the beach. They're going to play some volleyball. I'm going to be their cheerleader."

"That sounds like fun." But something about the way my sister said it made me wonder. Was one of these friends a boy? I was going to have to find that out later when my mom wasn't listening.

So many secrets. I didn't like it.

I wanted the old times. The simple times. The moments with my dad while I was growing up. When my family was whole and complete.

But there was no need to wish for things I'd never experience again. I had no choice but to move forward.

I finished eating and glanced at my watch. "I'm going into work for a couple of hours this morning."

"They're making you work on Saturdays too?" My mom gawked. "What kind of people are they?"

"You know Americans. Workaholics."

"I hope you won't become a workaholic too." My mom pressed her lips together, her gaze clearly full of concern about the influences of this culture on me.

She often reminded me about the Bible verse that spoke of the camel going through the eye of the needle more easily than a rich man getting into heaven. When all our needs were met, people rarely turned to God. Americans didn't realize how rich they were compared to the rest of the world.

"Don't worry, Mama," I reassured her. "I still like my quiet time. I just need to learn all the ropes at the job first. Then things will settle down."

My mom's narrowed gaze was still filled with worry. "Hold on to what's important to you. People can take a lot of things away from you, but they can never take away your character."

That's what I had told myself last night also. How did I reconcile who I wanted to be with how I'd been raised? Was it even possible?

"I will." I rose, put my plate in the sink, and kissed her cheek before stepping away. "I promise you, Mama. I will."

I grabbed my purse and started to step outside when my sister appeared beside me. After I closed the front door, Ruth turned to me.

"I know Driscoll and Associates isn't a law firm," she announced.

Some of the blood drained from my face.

"How do you know that?" I deflected my answer.

"I did some research. I got bored." She crossed her arms.

My sister was the one obsessed with American culture. I caught her on more than one occasion watching YouTube videos. Her style of dress was trendy. She looked at the world like a dog looking at a bone—she practically salivated to make it her own.

I lowered my voice. "I don't want Mama to worry."

She shrugged. "I know. It makes sense. And now I know why you're acting so weird. But you really do have a new look about you. It's almost like you're . . . living your destiny or something."

"Maybe I am. I never thought I would like doing something like this, but I'm glad I gave it a shot." I glanced around, looking for trouble as I remembered all the events of this week. The last thing I wanted was to put my family in danger. I'd never forgive myself if I did.

My sister squeezed my arm, sincere concern filling her wide-eyed gaze. "Just stay safe, okay?"

I reached down and squeezed her hand. "Don't worry. I will."

With that, I set off for work.

"Good job last night," Oscar told me as I sat across from him in his office. Michael also joined us. Our boss had called us in for an impromptu meeting as soon as we'd arrived, and I'd filled them in on the evening's events.

"I did my best." I shrugged, as I remembered what had transpired at the fundraiser. "It was kind of fun, to be honest. It stretched me. I felt like an anaconda who just realized it could eat a crocodile."

Both of the men stared at me, and I felt certain Oscar wanted to make another Dora comment. Maybe I should tamp down on my jungle references, as Michael had suggested.

"Almost dying can do that." Michael gave me a brotherly look.

Oscar continued. "Now we have to figure out who put the knife to your throat. Do you still think it was Bernard?"

I'd been thinking about that a lot. I shook my head. "I do feel like Bernard had the opportunity and means. The only thing is, if he framed his client for this murder, I'm not sure exactly what he would achieve."

"Me neither," Michael said.

"Besides, wouldn't Flash remember something if there had been an argument first?" I asked. "Before I came in this morning, I did a little more research online. I can't find any connection between Bernard and Sarah."

"Yesterday, I double-checked cell phone records and financial transactions for both Bernard and Sarah," Michael added. "I didn't find any connection between the two of them. I also talked to a few of Sarah's friends, and none of them seemed to think that Sarah and Flash had ever talked before that evening."

It looked like another dead end.

"I did see Flash at the fundraiser last night," I told them. "Not at the party. He was actually sitting in his car outside when I left. It was a little strange."

Oscar narrowed his eyes. "He told me he almost went but changed his mind. Not everyone treats him the same since all this happened. He probably just got cold feet."

That was a possible explanation. Or had Flash been there to keep an eye on me?

I cleared my throat, wanting to put everything on the table. "I should also tell you that there was a police detective there last night who ended up helping me."

Oscar's gaze narrowed. "Who was it?"

"Detective Hunter—"

"Detective Hunter?" Oscar's cheeks reddened. "You do

not share anything with Detective Hunter. Do you understand me?"

My eyes widened at the harsh tone of his voice. "I don't
know what you have against him, but he seems like a
perfectly nice—"

"He's not. He's incompetent. And he's the last person I
want you talking to. Do you understand?" His nostrils flared
as he stared at me, his voice still seeming to echo through the
room.

I knew better than to argue with him now. He was heated
and probably illogical.

I nodded before pointing to the door. I didn't want to be
in the room with the man anymore.

"I'm going to get back to work then," I said.

"But do you understand? Answer my question!"

I froze, my throat tightening. I didn't like being talked to
like this. I turned slowly and nodded. "I understand."

I exited Oscar's office and went to my desk. A moment
later, Michael sat down in the chair at his desk. Neither of us
spoke for a moment.

"Don't take it personally," Michael started, making no
move to start working. Still, he stared at his computer, almost
like he didn't want to give any hints that he was on my side
to anyone watching.

Or was he? I wasn't really sure.

I swallowed hard, trying to remain composed despite the
verbal lashing I'd just received. "Why does Oscar hate Detective Hunter so much?"

"I'm not sure of all of the details, but it goes back to when Oscar worked for the police department."

"You mean, before Oscar got fired?"

Michael nodded, still not making eye contact. "I'm not sure what happened. He doesn't talk about it, and I don't ask. But whatever it was, it had to be ugly. It turned Oscar's whole life upside down, and I think Hunter was somehow involved."

"It doesn't give Oscar the right to be so nasty." I frowned, remembering all those Sunday school lessons my mama had taught me about how I should treat others.

"I agree. Don't let this get you down. Oscar will get over it. So will you."

I turned toward Michael and lowered my voice. "Did I do the wrong thing by telling the detective the information?"

I wasn't sure why I asked the question. I'd already made my mind up that I'd do it all over again if in the same situation. It would be nice to know what kind of people I was working with here. Did we share the same viewpoints? I had my doubts—and those doubts made me uncomfortable.

"In most cases, police and private detectives do not work hand in hand. They do not get along. If you think the police are going to be your friend, you're wrong. You'd be wise to keep that in mind."

It was a good neutral answer. That was going to have to do for now, I supposed.

"Good to know." I turned back to my desk. "So, what do I do now?"

Michael glanced at his watch. "I promised Oscar I would

give him three hours today, and no more. This is my day with my daughter, and I don't want to waste it."

"That's understandable. So how can we use this time for the best?"

He leaned back in his chair and observed me. "I don't know. What do you think?"

I had a feeling this was a test. "Well, since you asked . . . something has been bothering me about the man who put the knife to my throat last night. There's something familiar about him, and I haven't been able to stop thinking about it since it happened."

"What seemed familiar?"

"Something about the way he spoke, the way he smelled. I just can't put my finger on it."

Michael straightened. "Sit down and do this: write a list of everybody we've met since we started this investigation. Nobody is too small. It could be the guy at the country club's guard house to the men golfing with Art. I want to see all of their names. You've got thirty minutes, and then we'll dig deeper."

I had been challenged. But Michael's idea seemed like a good one.

As Velma and Oscar left for breakfast, I picked up my pen and paper and got busy.

CHAPTER THIRTY

I did what I did best, and I made my lists. Yes, lists. I'd done the one Michael suggested and one that I came up with on my own. I even created them in Excel, which excited me entirely more than it should.

In the first column, I listed what I knew about the killer:

- He was near Flash's condo on the night of the murder.
- He was left-handed.
- He knew Flash used sleeping pills and probably drugged him.
- He's a big fan of Flash.
- He smelled somewhat familiar.
- He wore black loafers.
- Has a cut on his arm.

Then I made my list of suspects.

- Bernard Sutherland: He was left-handed, had the opportunity to make it back to Storm River in time for the murder. If he knew Sarah was trying to blackmail Flash, he could have stepped in, and things could have gone south.
- Art Smith: Best motive. If Flash went to jail, the endorsement deal was off. He'd save his company thousands, and he might even financially gain from that.
- Flash Slivinski: He'd been watching me at the fundraiser. Sarah may have threatened to blackmail him. In a fit of rage, he could have killed her and then pretended to black out.
- A competitor: Could someone we hadn't even considered be guilty?
- Emily Riviera: Jealous? Lied about seeing him that morning?
- Sarah connection: What if this had nothing to do with Flash and everything to do with Sarah?
- Damien:

I wrote his name down last, just in case. I mean, it was weird that he'd popped up twice during this investigation. But he'd been right-handed, and, as far as I knew, he had no connection to Flash. Right?

I deleted him from my list.

As I stared at my notes, I still didn't feel settled. What if the killer wasn't one of these people? What if we'd been looking in the wrong direction this whole time?

Out of curiosity, I did a couple quick searches, and I made one phone call.

My mind went back to the scent I'd smelled on the man. Why was it familiar?

My head jerked up as realization washed over me. Suddenly, all the clues that had been nagging at me flooded to the surface.

"I think I know who did it," I announced, disbelief emerging in my breathless voice.

Michael turned from his computer and faced me, his eyebrows forced together in doubt. "Just like that?"

I nodded, my thoughts still racing and sorting out my mental discovery. "If the man who assaulted me last night is the same one who killed Sarah, then I might have a name."

Michael still stared at me, as if humoring me. "Is there a way to prove your theory is correct?"

I nodded slowly. "I think there is. How do you feel about going for a ride in ten minutes?"

He glanced at his watch. "Can we be back in two hours?"

"Let's hope. I just need to make a few phone calls first. Okay?"

"Okay."

After my calls—which had been fruitful—we went to Michael's car. Actually, his minivan hadn't been fixed yet, and he was driving a decked-out Jeep Wrangler instead.

Michael opened the door for me, and I climbed inside. "It's my dad's. He bought it when he had a midlife crisis."

"It looks nice." There were very few material possessions I dreamed about owning. But I had a fond spot for Jeeps.

"It is nice. I'm borrowing it until my minivan is fixed." He closed my door and then hurried around to climb in himself.

I pulled on my seatbelt, my pulse pounding with anticipation. "Is the minivan even fixable?"

"I should hear back sometime soon. You know how it goes when insurance is involved."

"Yes, I do. Insurance is a blessing and a curse." Unfortunately, I knew that all too well because of my sister's illness.

"You can say that again."

I needed to figure out how this was going to play out. Michael and I had no authority to arrest this person. If we managed to get this guy to confess . . . how long would it take for the police to arrive? What if things turned ugly? Did Michael conceal carry? Should I think about getting my license to do so?

I had so many questions.

I was too new at this to know how to proceed. But maybe we should play it by ear.

I talked through my theory with Michael, and he listened quietly. I held my breath when I finished, waiting for his reaction.

He slowly nodded. "You might be onto something. I think it's worth checking out."

Relief washed through me. Good. I wasn't totally crazy.

A few minutes of silence fell between us as we continued down the road.

Michael glanced at me a second later. "So, last night you

got another glimpse of the social scene here in Storm River, huh?"

"That's right. And, once again, it proved to me that I do not fit in."

"That's not what Velma said." He raised his eyebrows.

I turned toward him. "What?"

He shrugged. "I wasn't the one who brought it up. But it was all Velma could talk about—how fantastic you looked in that little red dress."

I felt my cheeks heat. "She did a good job helping me to blend in."

"You know that if you're not comfortable in this line of work, there are jobs for you up in DC. The fact that you're bilingual, that you used to work for the government in Yerba, that you're intelligent . . . there are probably other things out there for you."

I drew in a breath at his advice. "Do you think I should quit?"

Did he think I wasn't cut out for this type of career? That I was doing a poor job?

Michael glanced at me and shook his head. "I didn't say that. I'm actually glad that Oscar hired you. But I also know that you've almost died three times since I've known you. That's got to be a lot for you to comprehend. Plus, you've got scruples. That's a blessing and a curse in this profession."

"This is all a little more than I expected," I told him. "But I haven't felt this invigorated in a long time."

"It's good you're being honest with yourself. But no one is going to blame you if you want to move on."

"I almost think you're trying to get rid of me."

His eyes widened with surprise. "Get rid of you? No, of course not. I'm starting to like having you around. I just don't want you to regret anything."

"I'll try to keep myself in check." I cleared my throat, trying to turn the subject from me to something else. Like Michael. "Sometimes, I'm surprised that you're still working for Oscar. You also have other skills."

He shrugged. "This keeps me close to my daughter here in Storm River. That's really all I want. I'm not much of a bureaucrat. Playing those games like they do up in DC? It's not my thing."

"I see." I pointed to an exit in the distance, realizing our chat needed to come to an end. "Right here is where we need to go."

I knew that in less than five minutes we were going to be at our destination.

I braced myself as I tried to figure out how things would go.

Michael and I walked into the Green Leaf Tavern and paused. Just as when we'd come the other day, the place was about a third full. TVs played in various corners and memorabilia hung on the walls.

But it was the person behind the counter who caught my eye.

The bartender. Zack.

Michael and I strode toward him, and I braced myself for the confrontation.

"You two are back again?" Zack said. Just as before, he dried some glasses. "By the way, I realized where I recognized you from. You're Michael Straley. You played three seasons with the Mets."

Michael pretended like he didn't hear him. "We have some follow-up questions."

"I told you everything I knew when you came in last time." Zack shrugged, appearing annoyed with his pressed lips and narrowed eyes.

I leaned closer. "Everything?"

His face grew paler, but he said nothing.

"What I'm wondering is if anybody else came in here talking about Flash?"

"People talk about Flash here all the time." Zack pointed to the walls. "There are pictures of him everywhere, and people know he likes to hang out here when he can. There's nothing unusual about that."

"But did you ever hear anybody come in and talk about a plan to ruin him?" Michael clarified.

The bartender's neurotic drying ceased as he looked at us. "I'm not sure really why you would ask that. It's a weird question."

"You seem to know a lot about him," I said. "Do you happen to know where Flash lives?"

"Another strange question. If you ask any of the locals around here, they'd be able to tell you the answer to that. It's pretty well-known where he lives." An edge crept into his voice.

"So I take that as a yes?" Michael said.

"I've heard rumors." Zack started rubbing the same glass again over and over.

I had a feeling that Zack had taken the job here precisely because Flash frequented this place.

"I happened to call your boss before I came," I said. "Turns out that the day Flash and Sarah were in here, you got off work a few minutes after they left."

He shrugged and put one glass away, only to grab another. "I'm not sure. I don't really remember."

"Maybe it was because you knew something bad was about to go down that day."

"Sounds like a stretch, if you ask me. But if my boss said I left shortly after, then I guess I did. I'm not sure what that proves."

I glanced at his arm. I knew the man who'd threatened me last night had cut himself when he'd hit Detective Hunter. That meant he probably had a bandage on his arm.

"Can I see your arm, Zack?" I asked.

Zack tensed and went completely still. "Why would you need to see my arm?"

"Just show her your arm." Michael's voice turned hard. "Unless you're trying to hide something."

"Of course, I'm not trying to hide anything." The man set the glass down and began to roll up his sleeve.

But before he finished, he grabbed the glass again and threw it at Michael. Then he took off in a run.

CHAPTER THIRTY-ONE

Michael blocked the glass before it hit him, and it bounced off his hand, shattering on the other side of the bar. Wasting no time, Michael sprinted after the man.

Zack was faster than I'd given him credit for. I followed behind and reminded myself that I needed to up my workout routine if I was going to stay in this line of work.

But as soon as I stepped outside, a new figure came into view.

Detective Hunter.

He stood on the sidewalk with his gun drawn and two officers—one of them being Bradford—beside him. Zack stopped in his tracks and raised his hands in the air.

I joined Michael near the door and soaked in the scene.

Detective Hunter paced toward us, his eyes still on Zack as Bradford handcuffed him.

"How did you know?" I asked him.

Hunter shrugged and glanced at me. "I didn't. I followed you. I wanted to see what you were up to."

"Is that right?" Today out of all days I hadn't actually noticed that I was being followed. Maybe I shouldn't give so much credit to my instincts after all.

"Do you want to tell me what you put together?" Hunter asked.

I stood by Michael, feeling some kind of strength through his presence. Then I launched into my theory. "I realized that Sarah had been in here talking with the man she was working with about how they would take down Flash Slivinski. They both knew what Flash had done, knew he was responsible for that hit-and-run. They wanted to get money out of him and ruin him."

"Keep going." The detective's gaze remained hooded as he waited.

I nodded toward Zack as he stood near the police car. "The bartender is one of Flash's biggest fans. It's why he started working here, if I had to guess. He overheard what they were saying and knew he had to do something. He didn't want to see his idol go to jail or have to give up his career."

"Okay . . ."

I swallowed my nerves before continuing. "I'm guessing that Zack also takes sleeping pills. It's a well-known fact that Flash uses them. I suspect Zack slipped a few into Flash's drink, thinking that if Flash passed out, he could somehow avoid what was to come."

"Keep going," Hunter said.

"But when Zack saw Flash leave with Sarah, Zack knew that the pills might not work. Sarah was about to blackmail Flash, and Zack wanted to stop her. My guess is that he had no intention of killing Sarah, but it just happened in the heat of the moment."

"Is that right?" Hunter called back to Zack, who stood by a police car.

He scowled. But his anger quickly crumpled into grief. "I didn't mean to do any of it. No one was supposed to die. I was trying to talk some sense into her. But she tried to leave. I grabbed her, and she fought back. I grabbed the knife from the butcher block and . . ."

He hung his head and sobs wracked his body.

"You followed me to the fundraiser," I continued.

"I needed a moment to talk to you alone," Zack said. "I just wanted you to figure out that Sarah was the bad guy, not Flash."

I guess he didn't give much thought to the fact that he'd also killed someone. He'd justified his actions, I supposed.

"How did you know it was him?" Hunter asked.

"It was the scent," I explained. "This place is known for its whisky. Not only does it smell yeasty, but there are also hints of vanilla and oak. We truly are what we eat—and we begin to smell like certain things. The scent of whisky had seeped into his skin and was eventually emitted through his pores. That's why you don't eat bacon before you go into the jungle. All the predatory animals will sense you coming—"

I noticed everyone staring at me again, and I stopped my blathering.

Hunter pulled his gaze away from me and turned back to Zack. "How did you know what Sarah was doing?"

"It's like the *Knives Out* girl said—I overheard Sarah and her friend talking," he said.

"I . . . don't have any knives on me." What in the world was he talking about?

"He means you look like someone who was in a movie," Michael whispered.

Hunter continued as if he didn't hear me. "Sarah's friend?"

"That's right," I said. "Sarah was working with someone."

"Who might that be?" Hunter stared at me. "Did you figure that out as well?"

"As a matter of fact, I did." I grinned. Then I pointed to someone in our circle. "Bradford did it."

Everyone turned to the officer.

His eyes widened, and he let out a strained chuckle. "Me? Why would I do that?"

"I checked. You were the officer on the scene the night of the hit-and-run. I made a quick call about it this morning. Sarah just happened to witness the accident, and she came to you with what she knew. The two of you came up with the plan together."

"Why would you think I knew Sarah?" he asked.

"You tried to scrub your social media of it, but I found a picture in the cache of the two of you together," I said. "You went to the same college. It's been a busy morning for me."

"That doesn't prove anything," Bradford said.

"I saw those cartoon cats in your police cruiser and assumed you liked felines. But then I realized they were from the card game Exploding Kittens. The waitress at The Board Room said a group always showed up to play that game, and it just so happened to be the same time she often saw a black sedan. A quick social media search showed me more than one picture of you with your car—one that looked just like the vehicle that hit Michael's a couple days ago."

Bradford's face grew paler. "That's ridiculous. Just because I play a card game and drive a dark sedan means nothing."

"I'm nearly certain you were the one who left the camera in Flash's condo," I continued. "You also left that threatening note on the BMW."

"Why would you think that?"

"The paper it was written on . . . it's the same kind found on the pads in the police station's supply closet. I saw them there when I was cleaning. I also saw your signature on the list inside that same closet. I assume you have to record whenever you check out things from the resource closet. I realized that the scrawl matched."

Bradford scowled but said nothing.

"And the night Damien got out of his handcuffs? It was because you let him out," I said. "You knew he was amped for trouble, and you saw him look at me with hatred in his gaze. Everything fell into place at just the right time because you also happened to recognize me from the video footage that you collected from the condo."

"Why would I collect video footage?" Bradford was trying to look cool, but his motions were becoming more jerky. His breathing looked shallow. His eyes flickered as he tried to process all of this.

In other words, we were making him nervous.

"Because you wanted to make sure no one found out what you'd done," Michael said. "You had to see who might discover your secret."

Bradford scoffed. "You don't have a lick of evidence to prove any of it."

"Except for me," Zack said. "I can ID you as the man who was with Sarah Vance that night."

Bradford's eyes widened again. He started to take off in a run when Hunter pulled his gun.

"Stay right there," Hunter growled.

Bradford stopped in his tracks and scowled. The other officer handcuffed him and began reading him his rights just as another police car pulled onto the scene.

Hunter turned back to me. "How did you put all that together?"

"It all started with the scent of whisky."

Hunter's eyes narrowed, either because he was impressed or thought I was over the top. "Very observant of you."

"I should be observant. My dad taught me to be vigilant. He said it might save my life one day."

"Well, I would say that he taught you well." Hunter offered a smile, one that actually looked sincere.

"I would say he did too," I said.

The look of approval the detective gave me made a

surprising warmth rush through me. I wasn't one to crave validation from other people, but right now it felt good.

Maybe I'd finally found something that I wanted to do—and that I was good at.

Maybe.

CHAPTER THIRTY-TWO

As Michael and I climbed into his dad's Jeep to go back to the office, all of my fuzzy, warm feelings began to fizzle. As my adrenaline wore off, reality hit me.

I remembered the struggles I'd faced over the past few days. I recalled my guilt. The fact I had to be sneaky. The reality that I couldn't even pray to God to help me because I knew He probably didn't approve of my actions.

Solving the case had left me on a mountaintop. But I couldn't rely on my emotions right now. I had to use my head.

I couldn't continue doing this. It had been fun. Investigating had been a thrill.

But I knew I was going to have to tell Oscar that I would be quitting.

As much as I'd loved doing this, I wasn't sure how I could

keep working this job and feel good about myself. The moral line I walked was too thin. Lying to my mom was too hard.

Maybe I'd wait until Monday to give Oscar the news.

Maybe.

"Good job back there," Michael said. "I think even Mr. Hard-to-Impress Detective Hunter was amazed."

"I don't know about that." I shrugged. "But thank you."

Just then, my phone buzzed.

I looked down, and I saw that I had a message from . . . Jono, of all people.

So how about that dinner date sometime?

Funny, I figured that he fed all the ladies at the gala those lines and that he would have forgotten about me.

I stared at the message for a moment, contemplating how I should respond.

I hadn't been out on a date since Sergio. But maybe it was time to start thinking about it. I'd put my life on hold for the last six months—that's when all the trouble in Yerba had started and when Sergio had broken up with me. I needed to start living again. Plus, I needed to figure out if Jono had some kind of connection with my past.

"Everything okay?" Michael glanced at my phone, a wrinkle forming between his eyes.

I held up my phone. "I just got asked out on a date."

His eyebrows shot up. "Is that right? With who?"

"None other than the one and only Jono." I braced myself for Michael's reaction. I knew he wouldn't approve.

"What?" Michael glanced at me, almost like he thought I was joking. "And what are you going to say?"

I shrugged. "I don't know yet. Maybe I'll say yes. Not because I think the two of us have a future together, but maybe because it would be a good start for me to get back into the world of dating."

His jaw flexed a moment until he finally said, "You can't fix him, you know."

His words caught me by surprise. "What do you mean? Who said anything about fixing him?"

Michael glanced at me again, concern in his gaze. "You're that kind of girl. The kind who will take on a guy for a project so you can help him through all of his problems. You can't make Jono a better person."

My eyebrows shot up this time. "You have strong feelings about him."

"You're a big girl. You can do what you want. But it's only fair to warn you."

I nodded, simply to show I was listening—not agreeing. "But just one date couldn't hurt anything, correct?"

Michael didn't say anything

I put my phone away. I would think about it. But, for now, Michael and I needed to give Oscar the update. Then I needed to get home so I could spend some time with my sister.

When I got back to my house two hours later, I found a note from my sister saying she'd left for the beach later than expected, so she was running behind. That was fine with me.

I could use some time to decompress.

I went to my room and sat on my bed. Maybe I'd read my father's next journal entry now. I could use a little of his advice.

My throat tightened when I pulled it out and turned to the right page.

I began reading:

I know this next part is going to take you by surprise. But if something happens to me, please know that it may not be an accident or from natural causes. My enemies are trying to find me, and I fear they get closer and closer every day.

I sucked in a breath.

My dad's heart attack might not have been a heart attack?

If someone killed him . . . I needed to find out who that person was.

That meant I couldn't quit the agency. I needed to learn all I could about tracking down the bad guys. Oscar wasn't the best in the business, but Michael might just be.

Tears flooded my eyes as I closed the journal.

"I'm going to do this for you, Papa. I'll find the person who did this to you."

ALSO BY CHRISTY BARRITT:

THE WORST DETECTIVE EVER:

I'm not really a private detective. I just play one on TV.

Joey Darling, better known to the world as Raven Remington, detective extraordinaire, is trying to separate herself from her invincible alter ego. She played the spunky character for five years on the hit TV show *Relentless,* which catapulted her to fame and into the role of Hollywood's sweetheart. When her marriage falls apart, her finances dwindle to nothing, and her father disappears, Joey finds herself on the Outer Banks of North Carolina, trying to piece together her life away from the limelight. But as people continually mistake her for the character she played on TV, she's tasked with solving real life crimes . . . even though she's terrible at it.

#1 Ready to Fumble
#2 Reign of Error

ABOUT THE AUTHOR

USA Today has called Christy Barritt's books "scary, funny, passionate, and quirky."

Christy writes both mystery and romantic suspense novels that are clean with underlying messages of faith. Her books have won the Daphne du Maurier Award for Excellence in Suspense and Mystery, have been twice nominated for the Romantic Times Reviewers' Choice Award, and have finaled for both a Carol Award and Foreword Magazine's Book of the Year.

She is married to her Prince Charming, a man who thinks she's hilarious—but only when she's not trying to be. Christy is a self-proclaimed klutz, an avid music lover who's known for spontaneously bursting into song, and a road trip aficionado.

When she's not working or spending time with her family, she enjoys singing, playing the guitar, and exploring small, unsuspecting towns where people have no idea how accident-prone she is.

Find Christy online at:

www.christybarritt.com

www.facebook.com/christybarritt

www.twitter.com/cbarritt

Sign up for Christy's newsletter to get information on all of her latest releases here: **www.christybarritt.com/ newsletter-sign-up/**

If you enjoyed this book, please consider leaving a review.